A Candlelight
Ecstasy Romance®

"ARE YOU TELLING ME YOU WON'T STAY FOR THE REST OF THE SUMMER WHILE I DIRECT THE NEXT PLAY?" NICK ASKED DISBELIEVINGLY.

"Yes," Darcy answered. "And this is the last time I can sleep with you."

"That doesn't make sense! You didn't sleep with me to further your career. You couldn't have been pretending that you loved me last night. I know it meant as much to you as it did to me. You were warm and loving, like a real woman."

Darcy shook her head, numb with pain. Nick's hurt and disappointment were torturing her, striking her dumb when she most needed to tell him the truth. But she'd lose him if she admitted her deceit. She wasn't Sheila Simmons, the scheming actress he'd fallen in love with, but her identical twin sister. Now she was caught, torn between living a lie and losing the man she loved. She threw on her dress and ran out of his cabin, sure that nothing worse could ever happen to her.

CANDLELIGHT ECSTASY ROMANCES®

STAND-IN LOVER

Barbara Andrews

A CANDLELIGHT ECSTASY ROMANCE®

Published by
Dell Publishing Co., Inc.
1 Dag Hammarskjold Plaza
New York, New York 10017

Dell ® TM 681510, Dell Publishing Co., Inc.

Candlelight Ecstasy Romance®, 1,203,540, is a registered
trademark of Dell Publishing Co., Inc., New York, New York.

ISBN: 0-440-18276-X

Printed in the United States of America

First printing—September 1985

To Our Readers:

We have been delighted with your enthusiastic response to Candlelight Ecstasy Romances®, and we thank you for the interest you have shown in this exciting series.

In the upcoming months we will continue to present the distinctive, sensuous love stories you have come to expect only from Ecstasy. We look forward to bringing you many more books from your favorite authors, and also the very finest work from new authors of contemporary romantic fiction.

As always, we are striving to present the unique, absorbing love stories that you enjoy most—books that are more than ordinary romance. Your suggestions and comments are always welcome. Please write to us at the address below.

Sincerely,

The Editors
Candlelight Romances
1 Dag Hammarskjold Plaza
New York, New York 10017

CHAPTER ONE

"Sheila, how can you ask me to do that!" Darcy looked into her twin's dewy eyes and remembered how easily her actress-sister could summon tears.

"I wouldn't ask if I weren't desperate!" Sheila dug into the depths of a huge red straw handbag and came up empty. "Do you have a tissue?"

"Yes, of course."

Darcy found a purse pack in the bathroom cupboard and returned to the living room, handing it over with a sigh. Her identical twin had been back in Springfield for less than an hour, and already their old pattern was reasserting itself: Sheila needing and Darcy supplying.

"When you called, I thought we'd spend the weekend together. Mom and Dad will be back Sunday from visiting Aunt Carrie, and they haven't seen you in ages." Darcy didn't try to hide her disappointment. As exasperating as Sheila could be, they'd always shared a special closeness: best friends as well as sisters.

Sheila patted her eyes, frowning at a smear of dark mascara on the tissue and glancing at her watch. "You know I'd love to stay, but I have to meet Tony Adler at O'Hare Airport tomorrow. I would've flown there directly from New York if it weren't for this summer stock contract. I'll be ruined if I back out now. Rehearsals start Wednesday."

"You agreed to it," Darcy said matter-of-factly. "From

everything you've told me, it's an honor to star in a play at the Duckeye Summer Playhouse."

"Oh, I suppose it is." Sheila paced the length of the sunny room, stopping to gaze at a massive fern hanging in the front window of her sister's second-floor apartment. "My plants always die."

"Because you're not home to take care of them."

"It's a silly name for a summer theatre," Sheila grumbled. "Just because the lake is shaped something like a duck's head . . ." Remembering what she wanted her sister to do, she changed the tone of her voice, forcing herself to sound enthusiastic. "But Mallard Lake is lovely, clean water and sandy bottom. Private too. All the summer people's cottages are on the opposite side. Behind the playhouse lodge and cabins there's a beautiful forest. You could gather enough pine cones to make Christmas wreaths for everybody in Springfield. You'd have a wonderful time there, Darce."

"I haven't been in a play since high school! I couldn't possibly pass myself off as you."

"We've traded places hundreds of times. Even Mom and Dad can't tell the difference if we're cagey about it."

"Sheila, we did that when we were kids!" Usually because her sister was in some kind of difficulty, Darcy recalled. "You're not a schoolgirl stuck with two dates on the same night anymore."

"No, this is much more serious. Tony Adler can open doors for me in Hollywood. I have a good shot at getting a part in a movie being cast right now. If I wait until the middle of the summer after the run of *Wings of Love,* I not only lose my chance in this picture, Tony will give up on me. Being in the right place at the right time is everything!"

"Then break your contract with the Duckeye Playhouse."

"And ruin my reputation? Equity actors just don't do that! And what if nothing comes of this trip to Hollywood? If I don't get a movie part, I really need the summer stock job. Do you know what my rent is in New York? Of course," she added quickly, "as long as you're filling in for me, you'll get the money."

"I'm not filling in for you! That's what I'm trying to tell you!" Darcy ran her hands over jet-black hair held back by two silver barrettes. The more she heard of her twin's hectic life as a fledgling actress, the more she appreciated her own orderly, calm existence. "I'm just not qualified, and even if I were, it's not the way I want to spend my summer."

"You finished your master's last summer, and you have nothing to do until school starts again."

Sheila was striking even when she sulked, her dark brown eyes set off by long lashes and gracefully arched brows in a heart-shaped face, but Darcy was immune to her sister's persuasive moodiness, ignoring the full lips set in a sultry pout. She'd seen Sheila practice this expression of simmering anger and disappointment in their big round dresser mirror too many times to be swayed by it.

"This is the first time I've ever had a summer completely free," Darcy said wistfully. "No graduate school, no camp job, no waiting tables or delivering phone books. Ten weeks of blissful vacation."

"With nothing to do!"

"I'm going camping with friends in August, and there are dozens of books I want to read. I need time to myself to relax, unwind."

"Sure, you have a job when school starts," Sheila said. "You don't know what it's like to be so uncertain about the future. You'll probably practice speech pathology right here in Springfield for the next forty years. I don't know if I'll have a job forty days from now, especially if you won't help me."

"You've had some good parts the last couple of years."

"Off Broadway, summer stock, a few commercials, all small stuff. I can be sued if I back out of the Duckeye production. I can kiss my career good-bye!"

Sheila sniffed again, this time convincing her sister that her distress was real.

"Even if I were willing to help," Darcy said, "I'm not qualified. I'm not an actress. Do you want me to stand in for you and make you look incompetent?"

"That's the beauty of this part! I'm supposed to play a deaf person. You wouldn't have to say a word, not one single word. Just stand around looking unhappy, and nothing can possibly go wrong."

"There has to be more to it than that." Darcy caught Sheila checking her watch again and wondered how much longer she planned to stay and argue her case.

"Nothing that you can't do," Sheila said. "After all your speech courses, you should feel right at home on the stage. And you know sign language; you worked two summers at a camp for deaf children. I had to learn enough to get through the part, and I've forgotten most of it."

"Three summers, but the last time was several years ago. I'm much too rusty to go up on a stage in front of people and sign my way through a part."

"The audience won't know if you make a mistake. Darcy, you're perfect for the part! You'll do it better than I did last summer in Connecticut. And the movie part could fall through. Then I'll be there before the play opens. You'll only be standing in for me at rehearsals. I have the script here." She pulled a yellow-covered playbook out of her bulging bag.

"Sheila, I don't think I should try to take your place. It's not as if we're still kids."

"Even then you were always worried about fooling people," Sheila replied. "I just don't see what difference it makes. We look exactly alike—or we would if you'd throw away those tacky barrettes and wear some eye makeup. We sound alike, and you know a lot more about deafness and sign language than I do. The Duckeye will be getting a better deal if you do the play instead of me. I got so bored with the

14

part last summer. All that time on stage and not a word to say."

"You must've done well. You were invited to repeat the role this year."

"Oh, my agent booked it. Sometimes he has no imagination at all. I begged him to find me a speaking part in another play so I could show my versatility. Maybe what I need is a new agent."

"Couldn't your agent handle the Hollywood offer?" Darcy asked, feeling tired and defeated under the onslaught of Sheila's arguments. She probably could fill in for her sister, she thought, but deceiving people was distasteful to her, not exciting and entertaining, as it was for her sister. Being an independent individual was difficult enough for an identical twin without trying to switch places and fill a role Sheila had created for herself.

"There isn't any offer, not yet," Sheila explained, forcing herself to sound patient and reasonable. "Tony can't be sure himself until I meet the people involved. He's honest enough not to promise me anything, but I have a feeling this will be the turning point, Darcy. I've never had anyone as important as Tony helping me."

"Why is he helping you?" Darcy was never comfortable hearing about her sister's complicated relationships with men, but she couldn't suppress her suspicions, and felt compelled to ask.

"He's crazy about me, of course!" Sheila laughed for the first time since entering the small but cheerful apartment, where the afternoon sun formed squares of light on the gold carpeting.

"Of course," Darcy said dryly. "Maybe his interest in you—"

"More than interest!"

"His affection then. Maybe he's being too optimistic, and you're giving up a good part for nothing."

"Oh, Darcy! You never take a chance on anything! How

can you look exactly like me and think like somebody's eighty-year-old granny? I'm surprised you left home long enough to go away to college."

"And graduate! I don't know how you could quit after three years."

"A degree doesn't mean a thing in show biz, darling!" Sheila trilled.

"I hate it when you try to sound like Joan Collins!"

"I never imitate other actresses!" Sheila was miffed, but she hadn't forgotten why she was there: "There must be something I can do to persuade you."

"The only thing you can do for me is spend more time with Mom and Dad. They do miss you, you know."

"I don't mean to neglect them." Sheila's conscience could be pricked. "I'm just so busy! Auditions, lessons when I can afford them, scrambling for commercials, hounding my pokey agent. The pace in New York is killing! I'd love to visit them and lie around all day doing nothing for a change, but I won't be young forever. In this business a woman is old at thirty! Do you realize I'll be twenty-seven in September?"

"I can remember our birthday." Arguing with Sheila always exhausted Darcy, possibly because she never seemed to win.

"The pay is really good for one week of performances," she said, and named an amount that surprised Darcy. "No one there knows me. The director's an older man, Julius Karnoff. He's supposed to be easy to work with. I always check out the director before I sign a contract. There's no real reason why you shouldn't do this for me, Darcy."

"It's unethical, impractical, and immature. Also it will spoil my summer," Darcy answered wearily.

"Why is it unethical? You'll do a wonderful job playing a deaf person. You've lived with them. And besides, no one involved in this production has ever met me before, so they'll never suspect that you're not me."

"Oh, Sheila . . ."

"Isn't it worth a few weeks of your time to save my career?"

Darcy only shook her head sadly, knowing her twin really didn't think there was anything wrong with the switch. To her it was a way of having her cake and eating it too; it wouldn't even occur to her that other people might be hurt by the deception.

"You're exaggerating," Darcy insisted. "You just have to make a career choice."

"I can't!" Sheila wailed. "If I don't show up, my reputation will be ruined. If I do, I may miss the best opportunity of my whole life!"

Darcy leafed through the script, reading a few lines at random from the middle pages. Could Sheila possibly be right? If it was as easy as her sister made it sound, maybe she was being selfish, refusing to help at this crucial time in her twin's career. Northern Michigan was lovely in the summer, and the playhouse was between Lake Michigan and the lush resort area of Grand Traverse Bay, not a terribly long drive from central Illinois. It wouldn't be a hardship to spend a few weeks in such a pleasant place.

"See," Sheila said, triumphantly pointing at the script, "you wouldn't have to say a single word. Just show up for rehearsals, and the rest of the time you can swim or lie in the sun. I'm the guest star, not some eager-beaver apprentice. No one expects me to paint scenery or sell tickets."

"That's not what worries me."

"Then what does?" Sheila located her spike-heeled bone-white shoes under the couch and slipped narrow, nylon-clad feet into them, straightening the skirt of a boldly-patterned red-on-cream silk dress.

"I don't have your style." Darcy tried to make it sound like a compliment. "I don't dress the way an actress does."

"There're no rules! In summer stock everyone wears jeans and shorts anyway." Sheila pouted again. "You're just making excuses."

17

There was some truth in her accusation. Darcy didn't know how to explain her feeling that it just wouldn't be right.

"Please, Darce, do this one thing for me, and I'll never ask anything else. Not ever!"

"I'm not so sure I'd be doing you a favor."

"Look, I'll make a deal. Go to the Duckeye Playhouse in my place, and I'll spend a full week with Mom and Dad before Labor Day. I swear it!"

"Even if you get a movie role?"

"No problem. The shooting won't start until September or October. And if the part falls through, I'll fly to Michigan on the first available plane. Maybe all you'll have to do is stand in for a few rehearsals."

"Oh, all right." Darcy felt as though she'd just signed up for summer camp in Siberia. "I'll do it, but I don't like it."

"Darling, I can't thank you enough!" Sheila hugged her exuberantly.

"Don't thank me until you hear how it turns out," Darcy warned dejectedly, wondering if Sheila ever listened to anything she didn't want to hear.

Driving her white Ford Escort north along the eastern shoreline of Lake Michigan, Darcy made the trip a leisurely one, stopping overnight in a small resort town and spending the late afternoon hours sunning on a public beach, lolling on the sunbaked sand, and almost forgetting her reluctance to go to the Duckeye Summer Playhouse.

Leaving the highway shortly before noon on Tuesday, she found the access road to Mallard Lake without any difficulty, driving inland, away from the sandy soil sprinkled with spiky grass. Slender-trunked pines, new growth planted on land that had been logged, lined the roadway, and freshly painted green and white signs assured her that the Duckeye Playhouse was just ahead. She wasn't disappointed by her first glimpse of the lake, a rippling sapphire gem under the bright sun with the lazy white sails of a boat sweeping across the far end. It was a small patch of inland water with the shoreline visible on all sides, narrowing into the distinctive bill shape that gave the lake its name.

If the round, red wooden playhouse had been moved from the shore to the weed-choked shallows southeast of the pier, it would indeed have served as the eye of the duck, with the white boards of the dock forming an unlikely eyebrow.

Darcy parked her car beside the sprawling rural structure, noticing that its rustic appearance was enhanced by freshly gleaming barn-red paint and new-looking gray shingles on the roof. Behind and connected to it was a low, squarish wing the same color. There was a spruceness and an air of anticipation about the exterior of the theatre that pleased her, easing some of the apprehension she felt about meeting the cast and crew for the first time.

The parking area for theater patrons was a large mowed field, staked out by white posts with round red reflectors nailed on them. To the northeast, a hundred yards or so beyond the theater, a long two-story lodge with no distinguishing architectural characteristics faced a double row of tiny cabins, all of the wooden siding on the structures weathered to a natural silvery gray. Beyond this cleared area the woods seemed dark and cool, the trees more massive and stately than the new forest she'd passed through driving there. So far Sheila had been right: it was a tranquil and inviting setting, with a narrow strip of sandy beach for the enjoyment of sunbathers and swimmers.

A young man, sprouting the beginnings of a straggly blond beard and wearing jeans and a T-shirt with a Michigan State logo, glanced in her direction as he hurried into the theater carrying a piece of poster board. His youth and his air of self-importance made her believe he was an apprentice, one of the do-all novices who were the slave-labor corps of summer stock, working more for love than money. The director, Sheila had assured her, was an older man, and

Darcy was hoping for a kindly father figure, a cross between Santa Claus and her Grandfather Simmons, who would patiently explain everything he wanted her to do.

The foyer, which circled the interior of the building, had a cement floor and a big glass case near the entrance to display the professional photos of the season's performers. She noticed Sheila's portrait under a grouping labeled as guest artists, then wandered to the left and retraced her steps to the right. The lobby surrounded the core of the building, except in back, where doors labeled PRIVATE led to the separate-but-attached wing she'd seen from the outside. Both doors to this work area were locked, so she climbed one of four short flights of steps, emerging to look down on the stage, a low platform in an arena setting.

"Oh, no!" she whispered to herself. "Theater-in-the-round!"

What else had Sheila neglected to tell her? This was no comfortable raised stage far-removed from the audience at one end of an auditorium. Instead, the metal reupholstered chairs salvaged from an older theater were bolted in tiers around the stage, so the audience looked down on the performers from all directions, save only for a gap where a wide, curtained entryway led to the backstage facilities she'd already located behind locked doors. If Sheila didn't come in time, she'd have to play the part surrounded on all sides by spectators. She didn't have the vaguest idea how to act in an arena theatre, but if the director was as nice as her sister had said, she still thought she could manage. What choice did she have now that she was there?

Stepping through the wide curtained doorway, she faced exactly what she'd expected: a large work area with curtained recesses on either side. The straggly-bearded young man had disappeared, probably through the rear exit, and Darcy assumed the absence of activity in the theater meant that lunch was being served at the lodge. Reluctant to go into the dining room while everyone was assembled there, she decided to wait in the theater and meet people a few at a time. Grand entrances were Sheila's style, not hers. Thank heavens no one connected with the playhouse knew her sister, she thought, or she'd never be able to stand in for her.

The backstage area looked like a hopeless jumble of equipment, furniture, ladders, stacks of wood, and odd bits and pieces, and Darcy could imagine how hectic it must be to have one play running while several others were in different stages of preparation. Some of the resident players might conceivably be involved in two productions at the same time, working from dawn till late night, acting one part and learning another.

Excited by the prospect of being involved in something so creative, she peeked into the first curtained recess, viewing a small, plank-walled dressing room with mirrored makeup stations on either side and a dress rack of costumes dividing the room in two. Did men and women change in the same room? she wondered. Actors were an uninhibited bunch, but she wasn't. It was a relief to find an almost identical facility behind the next curtained opening.

Making her way up one side and down the other, Darcy found the tool room, several miscellaneous cubbyholes, and the costume department. There were two sewing machines there, and the walls were lined with wardrobes. The last opening had a wooden door, and she turned the handle, expecting to find it as deserted as the others. When a man looked up abruptly from a desk where he was working, she was so startled she gasped.

"Sheila!" He looked as shocked as she felt.

"I thought no one was here," she managed to say.

"So, you decided to show up."

He rose slowly, staring at her with icy blue eyes. He had unruly mahogany hair, a rugged, tanned face, an aggressively square jaw, and lips tightened into a disapproving scowl. His expression nearly made her panic and blurt out

21

that she was Darcy, not Sheila, but she caught herself just in time, anger at her sister flashing through her mind.

Sheila had promised that no one there knew her!

"I *am* expected," she said tonelessly, not mistaking the angry challenge in the man's voice. Who was he?

"But you didn't expect to see me?" he asked, backing away a few steps and perching on the edge of a scarred wooden desk where he'd been working on a prompt book.

"Well, no." She moistened her lips with the tip of her tongue. "I didn't think I'd know anyone here."

He nodded, looking so grim she wanted to bolt away. What had Sheila gotten her into this time? There was so much accusation in his silent appraisal, she had to say something.

"Can you tell me where the director is?" She thought frantically and came up with his name. "Julius Karnoff. I should tell him I'm here."

"As far as I know, he's still in C.C.U."

Whoever this man was, Darcy thought, his hostile tone demonstrated that he was no friend of Sheila's.

"C.C.U.?" She'd heard those initials before but was too rattled to attach any meaning to them.

"Coronary Care Unit. Roosevelt Hospital in New York."

The kind and considerate director she'd been expecting had had a heart attack! She wondered if shortness of breath, clammy hands, and a rapidly pounding heart were signs that she was about to follow suit.

"You mean he won't be the director this summer?" she asked needlessly.

"Of course not," the man said impatiently. "Would I be here if Julius could make it?"

"No, I suppose not."

He kept staring at her as though he expected something from her. She didn't know his name, but it was clear that she was supposed to react to him in some way.

"Well, I guess we'll be working together then," she said,

22

using all her meager acting skill in an attempt to sound cheerful about it.

"I guess we will." His soft-spoken sarcasm was oddly painful to her; she didn't want this attractive stranger to be angry with her.

"Will it be a problem for you?" she asked hesitantly, probing for some clue to explain his hostility.

He laughed harshly. "I imagine that's the last thing you're worried about." He slid off the desk and moved closer, stopping less than two feet from her. "You are looking good; I'll give you that. You finally took my advice and stopped laying on purple eye shadow an inch thick."

Sheila had said something about eye makeup. But because no one at the Duckeye Summer Playhouse was supposed to know her twin, Darcy hadn't bothered to change her makeup or hairstyle, preferring to keep her long, silky hair out of her face.

"Those things in your hair will have to go, though," he said curtly, stepping closer and unfastening first one and then the other tortoise-colored barrette and handing them to her.

Dumbfounded by his intimate gesture, she stared mutely at her hair clips, completely at a loss how to act with him. That he knew Sheila well was obvious. He was also extremely displeased with her, and there was no trace of welcome in his face or words. Darcy edged toward the door, thinking only of escape. She longed to run to her car and drive away from this sticky situation, but even more she wanted to know who this man was.

Tall and broad-shouldered, his torso under a white net tank top was well developed but carried no extra weight. There was a threat in the forward thrust of his body, and his thighs strained the threadbare fabric of a faded pair of jeans. His size combined with his antagonism was intimidating, making her feel shorter than five feet five, and wholly inadequate. Darn her sister! There were no simple favors where Sheila was concerned!

"You must be shocked to see me here," he said. "I've never seen you at a loss for words before."

"I'm just surprised," she said weakly.

His laugh wasn't pleasant. "I'll just bet you are!"

"I can leave if you like."

"You do that," he said matter-of-factly, "and you'll have to buy a ticket to see the inside of another theater."

Darcy didn't know anything about him, but she sensed this was no idle threat. If she left now, Sheila's career would be ruined.

"You certainly don't want to work with me." She was feeling her way carefully, desperately eager to learn more about him.

"That's true." He seemed to be relaxing a little, leaning one hand on the back of an old oak desk chair. "But you're the one who has to worry about it, not me."

"Did you know I'd be here?"

"I checked out the schedule of guest actors before I agreed to direct."

"If you object to me so much, why did you come?"

"I owed some favors, and I needed a change of pace." He reached for the pocket of his tank top without thinking about it, then smiled with the first trace of warmth he'd shown. "I gave up smoking after you left me. Sometimes I still forget and reach for them."

Darcy's worst suspicion was confirmed: whatever lay between the director and her sister had been personal, not professional. Knowing this made her position seem much, much worse.

"It must be hard, giving up cigarettes," she said sympathetically.

For a minute she thought she'd goofed: he could've been a cigar or pipe smoker. She was supposed to know all about the man, and she didn't even know his name.

"There are harder things to give up," he said curtly, sitting down and scraping the cement floor as he pulled the chair closer to the desk. "You did *Wings of Love* in stock last summer?"

"Yes, in Connecticut."

"Not your usual kind of part?" He appeared to be studying the annotated copy of the script in front of him.

"No, I suppose not." No part in the world could be more difficult than confronting one of Sheila's ex-lovers.

Darcy felt even more glum thinking of the stranger in this way, and she wanted very much to believe she was wrong about the nature of his relationship with her twin. Maybe they had been friends who'd quarrelled or acquaintances who'd never become close. Maybe Sheila had provoked all his bad feelings by rejecting him right away. Focusing her eyes on his shoulders, the freckles barely visible under a deep tan, Darcy knew in her heart there wasn't a chance in the world that Sheila had held herself aloof from this man. Darcy could not, *would not,* work with him.

"It's not a difficult part. There must be someone in residence here who could play it," she said decisively.

"Not a difficult part!" He sprang up from the chair and grabbed her shoulders, looking so furious she expected him to shake her. "It's that kind of attitude that's holding you back, keeping you a bit player!"

Darcy squirmed under his angry stare, and she wasn't even guilty as accused!

"What's the use?" he said with disgust, backing off but not taking his eyes from her face. "You're never going to learn that there's more to acting than mouthing words and wiggling your fanny."

"That's not fair!" Darcy said with more spirit, defending her sister's acting ability.

Sheila would never be a great actress, but she had a nice comic touch and good stage presence, carrying out her roles with poise and confidence. Her voice was low-pitched but clear, ideal for sultry siren parts. Even in high school she'd put all of herself into her parts. Sometimes, in fact, the whole family became annoyed because she acted like her character offstage as well as in the production. When she starred in a summer stock production of *The Seven Year Itch,* she nearly drove them crazy imitating Marilyn Monroe's breathy voice.

"I don't know how your agent snagged this part," he said harshly, "but it's not your kind of play."

"You think I can't handle it?" Darcy asked aggressively, trying to meet this challenge the way her sister would.

"I wondered when you'd drop that meek-little-girl act. I imagine you'll muddle through the part with my help, but I'm not expecting much depth or insight."

"Isn't that the director's job, to get the best performances possible out of his actors?" She was furious now, sure that he wasn't giving Sheila a fair chance.

"You should know the play comes first with me," he said dryly. "If you have anything to give to the role of Beth, I'll get it from you. I'm just not optimistic."

"Great. A wonderful note of encouragement."

Sheila was always mentioning a "wonderful note of" something or other. Darcy was surprised at how easy it was to put herself in her twin's shoes when she was angry.

"Nick, do you want me to—"

The man she'd seen carrying the poster board shut his jaw with a click when he saw her. Up close he wasn't as young as she'd thought. Fine lines radiated out from the corners of his eyes, and his forehead was deeply creased. His gangly, unco-ordinated movements and nervous energy made him seem boyish from a distance.

"Our stage manager, Ken Davidson. Ken, I see that you recognize Sheila Simmons."

Darcy smiled warmly, doing her best to charm the stage manager when she greeted him. Working with one hostile

26

man was going to be bad enough; she needed all the friends she could find.

With a shock she realized she'd decided to stay. It was a crazy decision when all she had to do was tell the truth and he wouldn't want her. This Nick whoever-he-was was welcome to his terrible opinion of her sister, she thought, but Sheila didn't deserve to have such a biased critic belittling her talent. Family pride was more than enough to make Darcy determine not to let this director damage her sister's career. She even nourished a feeble hope that she could show him Sheila was a good actress. She had no idea how she'd manage to do that with her limited experience and meager talent, but at that moment, she was angry enough to try.

"I wanted to ask if you're planning a walk-through this afternoon," Ken said.

"Yes, I think we'd better go back to that for Sheila's benefit." Ken left and Nick turned to her. "The rest of the cast has been working here several weeks," he said. "They'll be ready when we open the season."

"But you're not sure I will be," she said in a soft voice full of challenge.

"We'll see. I called the rehearsal for three, so you have time to settle in. Cabin six is the guest house. You can pick up the key at the lodge from Mrs. Corning."

His curt words told her she was dismissed, and she turned to leave with relief, determined not to spend any more time alone with him.

"Oh, Sheila," he said, catching her arm as she turned to leave. "Welcome to the Duckeye."

He took her in his arms before she knew what he intended, kissing her roughly on her lips, then releasing her just as abruptly.

It happened in a split second, then he was gone, but in that instant Darcy learned something that shattered her confidence in deciding to stay. Nick didn't hate Sheila, as his harsh words seemed to indicate. Unguarded for just a moment, his face told her something entirely different and much more alarming: he cared very much for her twin.

Moving her car to a parking area between the lodge and cabins, Darcy walked into the building, attracting a few offhand "hi's" and uncurious glances as the crowd gathered for lunch scattered to different jobs. The main room was long and low, paneled in knotty pine and filled with Formica-topped tables and metal folding chairs. The only distinctive feature in the room was a large fireplace made of smooth boulders, the open hearth blackened from frequent use. All the room needed was a stuffed moose head to make it a typical summer-camp lodge.

In the kitchen she found Mrs. Corning, a stout, red-faced woman with huge upper arms who introduced herself as the head dietician. In fact, she did all the cooking, with the help of a couple of local teenagers, but she cherished the honorary title. After checking that Darcy wasn't "one of them that don't eat meat," she cheerfully handed over a ring with a key and a flat wooden marker for cabin number six. Mrs. Corning had little interest in actors unless they appreciated her Texas hot chili and New England pot roast.

"Pasties are my specialty," she told the newcomer, wiping her hands on a printed terry towel. "Thick flaky crust that melts in your mouth with diced potatoes and seasoned meat inside. Miners in the U.P., that is the Upper Peninsula, take them underground for their lunches wrapped in thick paper so they stay hot all morning. My father and his father, they both worked the copper. You want some lunch, dear?"

Darcy was too agitated from her encounter with Nick to care about food. What she did want was information.

"No, thank you. I'd better settle in right away. The director called a rehearsal for three o'clock. I guess he likes people to be on time. I wouldn't want him mad at me the first day."

"Mr. Cross get mad? I'll believe that when I see it!" The woman chuckled, brushing aside a springy cluster of hair.

28

"I've been coming here seventeen summers, and I've never seen a sweeter man in charge. Loves my cherry crunch. I can't wait till I can make it for him with the red sours fresh from the tree. Makes all the difference."

Darcy left with a quick thank you. If Nick Cross was a "sweet man," she was Sarah Bernhardt. Nick Cross, Nicholas Cross: the name sounded vaguely familiar, but she wasn't enough of a theater buff to know why. One thing was certain: Sheila had never mentioned him.

The cabin was clean and camplike with green and gold tiles on the floor, sunny yellow walls, and an iron bedstead painted brown. There was a space heater under one window and a tiny bathroom just large enough to allow the door to close when someone was in it. There was no tub, but the metal shower stall was newer than the rest of the cabin. Darcy had spent enough time at summer camps to know this wasn't a bad lodging. White nylon curtains covered two small windows that were also equipped with shades, and the cotton bedspread was an unstained white, worn but still fresh-looking.

She made quick work of unpacking; as an enthusiastic camper, she knew how to travel light. In only minutes the contents of her suitcase were inside a heavy oak dresser, the drawers lined with new white shelf paper. There was just enough room on an open clothes rack in a recess beside the bathroom to hang her garment bag and its contents.

It was fairly cool with an overcast sky that neither promised rain nor denied the possibility of it. Behind the cabin she could glimpse the lake through a grove of trees, but the window was too high to give much of a view. After changing into tailored navy slacks and a casual pink knit top, she located the script book Sheila had given her, but trying to read through it one more time was like reading underwater. She couldn't concentrate enough to make sense of the sentences. Giving up the effort, she sat on the edge of the bed, thinking.

29

One question was nagging at her: Did Sheila know about the substitute director? When did Julius Karnoff have his heart attack? From what Nick had said about rehearsals, it sounded as if he'd been there for several weeks. Of course, that didn't mean Sheila knew about the change. Darcy gave her twin the benefit of the doubt, at least for the moment, as nervousness about the first rehearsal pushed everything else from her mind.

CHAPTER TWO

Entering the theater from the rear, Darcy could hear some-one banging out a boisterous tune on a piano. The scene being rehearsed had nothing to do with *Wings of Love.* Dancers were stirring up dust as they followed the lead of a perspiring young man in gray tights.

"Where is *Wings of Love* rehearsing?" she asked the only person she recognized, the stage manager, Ken Davidson.

"In the lodge," he answered before reprimanding a young woman sitting in one of the theater seats, putting on dancing shoes. "Joyce, the call was for two thirty." Turning back to Darcy, he said, "Sorry no one told you. We rehearse *Carousel* here in the afternoon and at the lodge in the morning. *Wings* is just the reverse."

"How do you keep track of everything?" Darcy asked.

"Good question! I have an assistant for each production, but sometimes I feel like a rubber band stretched too far."

"Well, if I can help in any way . . ." It occurred to her it was a silly offer since she didn't know enough to be valuable to anyone, but he seemed to appreciate it.

Hurrying back to the lodge, Darcy gripped her script so tightly that her knuckles were white. A bold-faced clock on the far wall of the main room—more spacious now that the chairs and tables had been pushed along the walls—assured her that she wasn't late, but the rest of the cast were there ahead of her. Nick wasn't.

"Sheila, I'm Constance Hardin, your teacher in the play.

We're so pleased to have you with us. Nick said you played Beth in Connecticut last summer."

The woman who greeted her was an attractive black woman in her mid-thirties, tall and slender with thick black hair arranged in a mound on her head. Her smile was reassuring, but Darcy didn't know whether Constance was naturally cordial to everyone or sensed how terrified she was.

"I'm pleased to be here." Darcy glanced at the other members of the cast, standing and sitting while they waited.

"Nick will be here in a minute," Constance said. "He's taking a phone call in the kitchen. Let me introduce you."

The cast was small, allowing most of the resident players to work on the musical that followed their play. Brett Dwyer, dark and blunt-featured with youthful handsomeness, was playing the romantic lead who loved Beth but didn't know how to deal with her deafness. Cole Handley, silver-haired with pouches under his eyes and red veins showing on his nose, was her possessive, insensitive father. The only other parts were minor ones filled by three apprentices, Jeanette, Sue, and Raleigh. In spite of her apprehension, Darcy remembered all their names; it was a habit she'd acquired as a speech pathologist working in Springfield's elementary schools. She liked to be able to greet children by name if she saw them outside of their therapy sessions.

Nick's appearance startled her even though she was keyed up to confront him. He was one of those rare males who commanded attention just by being present, and she sensed an immediate alertness in the other actors, a straightening of postures and shifting of positions that indicated their readiness to follow his lead. He didn't speak directly to Darcy, but he did give directions for her benefit. The others had rehearsed the play so much they didn't need instructions to begin.

Using folding chairs to represent furniture and props, Nick outlined each scene, letting the players walk through their parts for Darcy's benefit without saying lines. Sure that she'd never remember which chair represented a table, a couch, or a park bench. Darcy moved sluggishly through the two endless acts, sure that she'd betray her ignorance by responding too slowly to Nick's directions.

The rehearsal was a disaster. Obviously the other players had expected much more from her. And when they began Act I, Scene I and she saw all of the other actors delivering their lines from memory, she nearly broke down in tears.

Much to her amazement, Nick was unfailingly patient with her, never once showing scorn or anger when she had to be told the most elementary things about stagecraft. She looked away from cast members when they were speaking lines to her, broke character to sneak a longing glance at the clock, flubbed several times when she was supposed to use sign language to answer Beth's teacher or father, and backed away when the actor playing her lover tried to embrace her.

When Nick finally called a halt, everyone was in a rush to leave, avoiding eye contact with her and making lame excuses not to linger.

"I was terrible," she said softly when only she and Nick were left in the dining room.

He started to reach for the nonexistent pack of cigarettes again, then stopped himself. "I'll take the blame for this afternoon. I shouldn't have cut you down like that the minute you got here."

It was the last thing she'd expected him to say.

"I've forgotten a lot since last summer," she said, knowing Sheila would invent some alibi. She'd never felt worse about herself, and Nick's consideration was unbearable, pricking her conscience like a bramble bush.

"It'll come back. I'm sure you did well then." His face looked dubious, but he was making an effort to sound positive.

There was nothing to come back to her, and she was sure she'd never be professional enough to perform with the polished players in the cast. Now was the time to admit the deception and leave with the shattered remnants of her pride. She tried to find the right words to confess to Nick but couldn't force herself to admit the truth. He was looking at her so intently she wanted to hide.

"I'm puzzled about one thing," he said slowly.

"What?"

"You're nervous. I thought I knew all your moods, but I've never seen you this edgy. I can't believe I have that much effect on you."

"Just an off day," she said flippantly.

Her voice sounded hollow and unfamiliar, and she knew it was because Sheila was speaking through her. Changing places with her twin had never been fun for Darcy; now it was promising to become a nightmare.

"I suppose I should be flattered that you care enough to let my criticism get to you." He smiled ruefully. "After eighteen months, I didn't know until I saw you how angry I still am."

"I suppose you have good reason." Darcy spoke for herself then, trying to remember what her sister had been doing a year and a half ago. Where and how long had she known Nick?

"You're full of surprises today," he said softly, standing less than five feet away and never taking his gaze from her face. "You'll have me believing that you've changed."

"Matured maybe." Darcy moistened her lips, knowing she'd goofed. Sheila would never admit that anything she did was childish or ill-advised.

Nick shook his head skeptically. "Sheila, if this is a new act you're putting on for my benefit . . ."

His voice trailed off, but the implied threat was chilling to Darcy. She was playing a dangerous game, and she didn't have a clue to what the rules were. She shrugged her shoulders, a gesture typical of Sheila, and asked a practical question.

"Do you have a rehearsal schedule?"

"Ken will give you one, but you're going to need more time than I expected."

"The Connecticut theater wasn't in-the-round." She had to offer some kind of explanation for her ineptitude.

"No?" He sounded surprised. "Well, I've never been there."

That, at least, was a relief.

"You're going to need some extra coaching then. Damn, time is always so short in summer stock. Tonight Harve is working with the chorus on stage, but they should be done by ten or so. Meet me then, and I'll go through the blocking with you on the stage. I want you to feel comfortable with what you're doing so we can make some progress with Act One tomorrow."

"You're going through the whole play with just me tonight?"

"Look, Sheila," he said, mistaking her question for a protest, "I know it means late hours but we're on a tight schedule."

"I wasn't worried about that—about working late." She nearly stammered in her discomfort, imagining herself alone with the director.

"I always thought you were a night person," he said, watching her through narrowed eyes. "Dinner's served at six. I'll see you tonight."

Even if she could manage to play the part, she didn't know how to react to the director. What had happened between Nick and her sister? She couldn't ask him, but Sheila owed her an explanation. Back in the cabin she had the name of the hotel where her sister was staying. Before the ten o'clock rehearsal, she absolutely had to talk to her twin.

The only phone in the lodge was in the kitchen, where Mrs. Corning gave her a cheery hello but made it plain that she didn't want idle visitors in her territory during the pre-dinner rush. There was no possibility of calling Sheila from there.

After locating the slip of paper on which she'd written the name of her sister's hotel, Darcy hurried to the theater, knowing the box office had to have a phone to book reservations, but to her disappointment, it was locked. A quick search of the lobby and backstage work area convinced her that the only other phone was the one she'd noticed on the director's desk. The door to his office was closed, and she knocked timidly, hoping against hope that he wasn't in.

"Come in." His voice came through the solid wooden door loud and strong.

Her first instinct was to run, but wouldn't she look silly if he came out and saw her? Inching the door open a crack, she said, "I only wanted to use the phone. I'll do it another time."

"You can use it now." He gestured toward the paper-strewn old-fashioned desk where a compact tan push-button phone looked out of place.

"No, it's not important. I'll do it later."

He stood, not trying to conceal his curiosity. "Is it a call you don't want me to hear?"

"Of course not! I just don't want to disturb you."

"I don't mind. Make your call," he challenged.

"Later tonight would probably be a better time anyway." Caught in the same situation, Sheila would come up with a clever excuse; Darcy was too flustered.

"Who is he?" Nick didn't quite succeed in sounding indifferent.

"Actually, I want to call my sister. She's on vacation in California."

He laughed at her statement, truthful as far as it went.

"Go ahead. I'm certainly not interested in your family secrets." He sat back in the desk chair and moved the phone to the edge closest to her.

"Later," she insisted.

"Any time," he said, his face telling her that he didn't for a moment believe she wanted to call a relative.

Dinner was trying, not because the cast and crew were unfriendly but because they weren't. They included her in the general conversation with the ease of people who have an all-consuming interest to share. In their case the talk concerned theater. Occasionally they touched on other topics, the weather, the economy, the baseball scores, but never for long. These people thought, worked, and lived the theater, a love affair that totally engrossed them. Darcy was fascinated by the vast store of experience behind even the apprentices, but she was at a loss to contribute much. Everything she knew about the world of drama came to her secondhand from Sheila. She was forced to be a quiet listener, hoping the others wouldn't interpret her reserve as snobbishness. To cover her lack of experience, she pretended to listen to Cole Handley with rapt attention, even though she thought the man cast as her father was the least likable person present. The ego of the man was astonishing; his stories were witty and entertaining, but all of them were a clever form of bragging.

In contrast, Nick was quiet, listening attentively to Constance on his right and Harve, the assistant director, across from him. He was at another table, but their eyes met once, creating an uncomfortable moment for Darcy. He was too interested and too perceptive. Did he know Sheila had a twin sister? This was only one of the questions she had to ask her sister.

The office was unlocked and empty after dinner, and Darcy placed a credit card call after getting the number of the Los Angeles hotel from information. She didn't know the room number.

"Sorry," a high-pitched woman's voice said. "We don't have a Sheila Simmons registered."

"Try Darcy Simmons."

Maybe her sister had carried out the deception on her end too. After a long pause, the same woman gave her another negative answer.

37

"I know my sister's staying there. She had reservations." Reluctantly she tried another name. "Do you have a Tony Adler registered?"

This reply came more quickly. "Mr. Adler checked out before noon today."

"Thank you."

Darcy felt betrayed, but wanting Sheila to have an innocent reason for her disappearance, she wondered if Sheila were through in California and on her way to Michigan. This seemed unlikely. Surely she'd warn Darcy before coming to the Duckeye so both of them wouldn't be seen at the playhouse. More likely, she thought, her sister had been invited to stay in someone's home or had moved to a more convenient hotel without bothering to tell her. There was no point in calling their parents in Illinois. They probably wouldn't know where she was, and they'd only worry.

Darcy dropped the receiver in disgust; she'd never felt quite so put out with her twin. Considering the tremendous favor she was doing for Sheila, she could at least keep in touch.

Choosing a top-row seat at random, she sat and tried to study the script while the *Carousel* cast rehearsed below her. The script's cover was dog-eared from her diligent study, but she couldn't seem to get a grasp on the part. Did Beth's deafness make her afraid of life, or was she self-sacrificing, not wanting to burden the man she loved with her handicap? Darcy would've loved to discuss the play with Nick, but to do so would make it obvious that she'd never done the role in Connecticut.

The only thing that didn't worry her was the sign language. She remembered more than enough to sign the simple responses required in the play. In fact, she already had them memorized, knowing her silent part as well as the other players knew their lines. It was the complexities of Beth's character that eluded her: How did the deaf young woman really feel about her lover, her teacher, and her father?

Darcy wanted very much to make a success of the part, not for Sheila's sake but for her own satisfaction. Until she captured the emotional makeup of Beth, Darcy would only be walking through the scenes like a wooden puppet, probably not even doing that well since theater-in-the-round made her terribly uneasy. No side of her would be hidden from the audience; she had to be totally involved in the part or she'd fail miserably.

Concentrating on the play, reading and rereading her important scenes, she barely noticed when the rehearsal below her started to wind down. The thud of Nick's rubber-soled Nikes on the wooden risers did catch her attention, and she watched with mild dread as he made his way to a seat beside her.

"They'll be out of here in a few minutes," he said.

"Yes, well, I think I'm ready," she said, then remembered that Sheila was never hesitant about anything. "I am ready."

"We'll go through the blocking again, and I want to run through Beth's scenes with David."

"Oh, Brett's coming then?" she asked, very much hoping the actor playing her lover would join them.

"No, I think we can work out some of the kinks without him."

Darcy knew a third person would make their rehearsal much safer, but she wasn't disappointed. Although usually happier not knowing about her sister's romances, she was very curious about this man from Sheila's past.

"I do know my part," she said, wanting to seem less incompetent. "All the sign language."

"Really?" He raised his brows skeptically, calling her attention to expressive blue eyes fringed by long dark lashes, unblinking as he studied her face. "I would've bet you'd fake most of it."

"There might be deaf people in the audience."

"True, but I still didn't expect you to go to that much trouble for a part."

39

"Actually, I worked at a camp for deaf children."

"Oh?" He looked even more disbelieving. "That's a surprise."

"My sister talked me into it. She's a speech pathologist in Springfield now. I needed the money, so I went with her."

Performing on stage couldn't possibly be as difficult as remembering to act like Sheila. Before she'd agreed to come to the Duckeye, she'd never really faced how different they were. How could she spend two and a half weeks pretending she was Sheila when Nick knew her sister so well?

The last of the performers were leaving, and the balding, owl-faced man who'd been playing the piano for rehearsals waved up to Nick and called, "Good night." Harve, who was directing the musical, summoned Nick for a hasty conference, then Darcy was alone with him on opposite edges of the low, circular platform that served as a stage. The thick, taut canvas underfoot was a nondescript gray with just enough give to remind her it wasn't an ordinary floor, and the houselights were off, leaving an oasis of hazy light in the center of the theatre. The curtains across the entry had been pulled aside to allow some air to pass through from the open outer door, and she could detect the faint aroma of pine and grass in the evening air, a clean fragrance that stirred the sluggish heat built up during the day. Giant wooden fan blades suspended from the high ceiling hovered over the seats like the wings of giant insects and kept the air moving, making the interior tolerable. There was no air conditioning; making a profit on summer theater was a chancy business, and owners tried to keep their costs down. The Duckeye had one advantage: its location in the midst of a resort area, which ensured large enough crowds to warrant running a play a full week and an extra weekend.

"Let's take it from the top," Nick said. "I'll read all your cues. In Scene One the piano can be the desk, and over here the bench is the chair you sit on."

He positioned these pieces along with several folding

chairs, and Darcy tried to remember where she belonged among all this makeshift furniture.

"When will we use the real set?" she asked.

"Beginning Monday. Tech rehearsal is Wednesday and full dress Thursday." His voice told her she should have known that from the schedule Ken had given her.

The scene should've been easier here on the stage with no other actors watching, but it wasn't. Darcy was so aware of Nick, constantly wondering about his reaction, that she couldn't concentrate.

"I've never seen you so stiff," Nick said in the middle of the second scene. "I'm not going to bite."

"I know that!" It was Sheila snapping back but Darcy who was miserable.

"Let's take a break and do a little stretching," he suggested, unbuttoning a faded blue plaid shirt he'd been wearing with the sleeves rolled to his elbows and tossing it on the piano bench. "Come on."

His chest was smooth and deeply tanned, the muscular swells proving that a man didn't need to be hairy to be emphatically masculine. With his legs wide apart, he reached upward with his arms, limbering up and obviously expecting her to follow his lead.

"That's it, loosen up," he said, touching the cloth floor with his finger tips, pivoting then arching his back.

The pull made his jeans slide low on his narrow hips, revealing a band of lighter skin, and Darcy had to look away. She was finding it surprisingly painful to imagine Nick with her twin, the two of them enamored and involved.

He stopped and watched her, making her too self-conscious to continue the stretching exercises.

"I think I know what's wrong," he said, stepping behind her.

For a moment his hands were warm and gentle on the back of her neck, then he began massaging, spreading his fingers over her shoulders and down her spine, strongly

41

kneading away the tension in the muscles but not the apprehension in her mind.

"Relax," he ordered. "You feel like you're wrapped in a straitjacket."

"I'm trying," she murmured, loving the feel of his hands even though they did nothing to remove the cause of her tension.

"Sheila, don't let the past interfere with this play. It's over between us," he said woodenly, walking over to retrieve his shirt and put it on. "We're working together, that's all. The only demands I intend to make are professional ones."

Stepping in front of her, he coolly appraised her.

"I won't deny I was hurt when you ran off without a word. Mad too. When I saw you today, I remembered how furious I'd been. But it didn't take me long to figure out there wasn't any future for us. Your idea of getting ahead isn't for me. I'm sorry it's over, but it was inevitable."

When she didn't answer, he said, "There's no reason why we can't be professional about working together."

The next scene did go better. She felt unaccountably pleased that there was nothing between her sister and Nick anymore. If she could tell him she was Darcy, not Sheila—but no, it would be silly and pointless to let herself be interested in a man who would disappear from her life after *Wings of Love* closed.

Finally concentrating on the part, she managed to get through another scene without any major blunders, but she hadn't counted on acting out the first love scene with the director.

"Use the piano bench as the park bench," he said, waiting until she was seated to come up behind her.

The part called for David to confess his love standing behind her, forgetting that Beth couldn't read his lips when she couldn't see him. Darcy didn't have to pretend shock when Nick's hands slid over her shoulders and came to rest on her breasts.

42

"You still feel good," he said in a husky voice, and Darcy knew this line wasn't in the script.

She automatically spun around in exactly the way the script indicated, but she wasn't acting when she pushed his hands away.

"Don't, Nick!"

"You're out of character," he said dryly. "You've been doing that a lot today—on and off stage."

"I don't think the script calls for you to be so fresh!"

He laughed, genuinely amused. "Fresh! I didn't know that word was in your vocabulary."

"Well, you know what I mean!"

"No, you have me totally confused. In the three months we were together, I completely forgot you grew up in the midwest, Land of Lincoln, home of Honest Abe, but your sophisticated veneer seems to be cracking. Maybe I don't know you as well as I thought."

"Maybe not." She was on the edge of panic, sure that he suspected something. "Can we get on with the play?"

"My pleasure," he said ironically, finding the place in the prompt book where they'd left off. "I think this is the part where I kiss you."

"Where David kisses Beth," she said quickly. "We don't need to practice that."

"No?" He sat beside her on the bench, his hip crowding hers and his leg pressed against her thigh. "I disagree."

With one hand behind her head, he slowly covered her mouth with his, ignoring her hands pushing against his chest until he'd kissed her thoroughly enough to take her breath away.

"That was no stage kiss!" she gasped, standing and retreating a safe distance across the stage.

"Stage kiss! If I didn't know better, I'd swear you came here straight from your high school's senior class play." His laugh didn't take the edge off his surprise.

"If you're not serious about rehearsing, I'm going to bed," she said with a flash of temper that was typical of Sheila.

"I'm not serious? You're the one who's pulling all these amateur tricks on me. If you think I'll fire you just because you're pretending to be incompetent, you're dead wrong, lady. You have a contract for a performance, and I'm going to get one out of you, one way or another." He stood with his hands on his hips, staring her down with stubborn insistence.

"You can start by skipping the love scenes. I'll do them with . . ." She was so angry she forgot the male lead's name. ". . . with the actor who's playing the part."

"Fine, if you do them with some touch of professionalism. At the afternoon rehearsal this scene was about as sexy as a goldfish kissing the side of his bowl. When David comes up behind you, you're startled, but your face shows your pleasure the instant you see him. He doesn't force you to kiss him. You're eager!"

"I'll be eager," she assured him crossly.

"Okay, try it again," he said, gesturing at the bench.

If she refused, she might as well go home. Sheila was an actress; she wouldn't hesitate for a moment in rehearsing a love scene, even if the actor involved had all the appeal of King Kong. Even though Darcy was angry with her sister, she'd given her word to take her place in the play. To do anything else would jeopardize her sister's future. In the close-knit world of the theater, Sheila's reputation would be sure to suffer irreparable damage.

Sitting on the bench, Darcy took in large gulps of air to prepare herself for the rest of the scene. She didn't have to pretend to be startled. Nick's hands came down on her shoulders like the talons of a hawk, making her flinch. When he sat beside her, his hip again crowding hers, she was quivering with anticipation, raising her face to meet the long, sweet kiss he bestowed on her. Mindlessly she responded with a warmth that surprised both of them, considering their recent words, letting her hands creep around the back of his neck.

They finished the scene, but Nick seemed subdued, saying nothing else about the way she was interpreting the part.

"I think that's it for tonight," he said abruptly.

"I thought we were going through the whole play." She should have been relieved by the early dismissal, but instead she felt an irrational stab of disappointment.

"You were right," he said brusquely. "It would be better for you to rehearse with Brett."

"I don't understand."

"You damn well do! I said there was no future for us. That doesn't mean I wouldn't like to go to bed with you again."

The word *again* hurt more than she believed possible.

"Well, that won't happen," she blurted out, strengthened by her own vehemence.

She wasn't Sheila! In college, she'd been in love and had a heartbreaking affair with a man whom she'd hoped would become her fiancé. But as graduation approached, he realized he wasn't ready to settle down, and when they parted he'd felt relieved while she was left devastated. Today Darcy knew quite a few men as friends, fellow teachers and those she met through a camping and hiking club, but she was totally uninvolved romantically. She knew she couldn't handle sex without love and commitment, and meeting the right man seemed like something that happened to other women, not her. The way she felt about Nick at this moment was temporary madness, Darcy told herself. Pretending to be Sheila was nerve-racking enough without becoming infatuated with her sister's ex-lover.

"Wait until I turn out the lights, and I'll walk you to your cabin."

"That's not necessary."

"Wait, Sheila!"

It was a command, compelling and completely unlike his usual tactful suggestions. What would Sheila do? She'd get sarcastic and storm out. But Darcy knew she wasn't a good enough actress to do that. She waited meekly, hating herself because she really did want Nick to walk her back to her cabin.

They made their way cautiously in the near-dark, guided only by a single light on a pole near the lodge. At the door of number six he stopped.

"I was out of line. I'm sorry."

Obviously it cost him a great deal to say this, Darcy thought. "Maybe you should replace me," she said. "It can't be easy for you, having to direct me." She remembered too late that Sheila would never say anything like this.

"Reverse psychology, sweetheart?" he asked sarcastically. "Are you trying to get me to fire you? Maybe you've had a better offer?"

He was so close to the truth that Darcy flushed with embarrassment, disliking Sheila's charade and hating herself for going along with it.

"No, I'll do the play if that's what you want." She tried to make herself feel less guilty by throwing the decision on to him, but it didn't ease her conscience.

"It's what I expect, that and a half-way decent performance."

"I'll do my best," she promised solemnly.

"For some crazy reason I believe you."

He stroked her cheek with the backs of his fingers, a touch as light and fleeting as the wings of a butterfly, but it told her enough to make her doubly miserable. Nick had cared deeply for her undeserving sister, and there was nothing she could do to make it up to him. Maybe it was time she stopped soothing the feelings of people Sheila had hurt, she thought, including her parents, who often were wounded by her twin's offhanded neglect.

"Good night," he said softly, rapidly walking past the row of cabins to the one closest to the theater and disappearing inside.

46

Later, lying sleepless on the unfamiliar, lumpy bed, Darcy tried to find excuses for her sister. It wasn't easy being an identical twin, sharing everything including appearance, although their parents had never dressed them alike or pushed them into the same activities. Sheila was the restless, aggressive one, craving the limelight. Probably she couldn't help it any more than Darcy could be held responsible for her more reserved, conservative nature.

It was her own fault, Darcy decided, that she was here in Sheila's place. She was overly protective of her sister and had to admit that she'd come partly to manipulate Sheila into visiting their parents. Maybe this terrible fiasco was just what she needed to finally cut the cord between them, to let Sheila be herself and bear the consequences when she was wrong.

None of this was any help in confronting the problem at hand: She still had to finish the play because she'd agreed to do it. Working with Nicholas Cross was going to be an incredible strain, but not because he was demanding or unreasonable. Under the circumstances, he was fair-minded, kind, and considerate. The brief glimpse she'd had of his warmth and tenderness made her very much afraid of her own feelings. How terrible if she fell in love with a man her sister had rejected!

CHAPTER THREE

The playhouse workday started early, which suited Darcy fine. She was a morning person, while her twin loved late evenings and lying in bed till noon. She dreaded continuing her impersonation, knowing that Nick was familiar with Sheila's habits and personality.

Even getting dressed to rehearse was a problem. Sheila never wore jeans, deciding in high school that skirts were more flattering, the shorter the better. The morning air coming through the two small screened windows was cool, but Darcy slipped into bright yellow shorts, expecting the day to grow warmer. A simple V-necked white knit top wasn't exactly her sister's style either, but she didn't own a showy wardrobe like Sheila's.

Automatically sweeping back her hair with long gold barrettes on either side, she glanced in the mirror and changed her mind. Hair clips were definitely out, and it wouldn't hurt to use a little of the dusky violet eye shadow she'd purchased at a drug store on her trip north. She wouldn't layer it so heavily that Nick noticed. Just for good measure she put some mascara on her already dark lashes and vigorously brushed her gleaming black hair. Small-boned and only average in height, she had the same slim waist and rounded hips as her sister, with full breasts and well-proportioned legs. Unlike her sister, she loved physical activity, keeping in shape by exercising and hiking, her favorite recreation. Sheila had been a wicked competitor in high school tennis but gave it up in favor of dramatics, keeping her weight down now by bouts of crash dieting.

Breakfast was available for several hours, with cast and crew wandering in at will to help themselves to a buffet kept warm in steam pans. Darcy met Constance on the way to the lodge and was glad to see a friendly face first thing in the morning.

"You're staying in a cabin too?" Darcy asked.

"Yes, so are Ken, Harve, and most of the equity actors. And Nick, of course. I don't know if the beds are any better than the lodge's, but there's more privacy."

The two women entered the dining hall and helped themselves to scrambled eggs, cereal, toast, and fresh strawberries, passing up coffee in favor of tea and pretending not to see the sticky pecan rolls.

"I always gain weight in the summer," Constance admitted.

"Have you been here before?"

"No, this is my first summer. Until a year ago I was a college professor."

"You're not anymore?" Darcy led the way to an unoccupied table, pleased to have breakfast with the woman who was playing her teacher.

"No, I gave it up for show business." Constance's laugh was rich and throaty.

"Where did you teach?"

"Halsted College, a small liberal arts school in Wisconsin."

"Let me guess. You taught speech and drama."

"Head of the department, actually." Constance smiled again. "In fact, I was the department, except for one part-time assistant."

"You're more daring than I am, giving up teaching for the theater." Realizing that Sheila would never say that, she quickly added, "Not that I could teach anything. What made you leave the college?"

49

"A chance to tour in *Wings of Love* with a national company."

"So you really know this play well."

"I've lived with it from Baltimore to Des Moines! I'm looking forward to being in one place all summer."

"Was the other director's interpretation much different from this one's?" Darcy desperately wanted to ask the experienced actress how the part should be played, but she was afraid of sounding ignorant.

"Every director and cast bring a little something different to a play, but Nick is very good. He has marvelous insight. Even after a year on the road, I'm still learning from him."

"How do you see Beth? Why can't she make up her mind to go away with David?"

"Her motivation?" Constance thoughtfully chewed a bite of toast and sipped her tea. "Fear, confusion, shyness. Imagine being born deaf and sheltered by an autocratic parent, never fending for yourself outside of your father's home and the School for the Deaf."

"David is offering her too much all at once?"

"Yes, and Beth has to be sure he won't do what her father did—suffocate her with love. David doesn't seem to understand her problems. He's not at all like her father, but he is possessive in another way."

"He doesn't really accept her handicap," Darcy said.

"That's the thing that worries Beth," Constance said thoughtfully. "Her father has no idea of what it means to her to be deaf. He treats her like a cripple. Until she's sure of her own potential for growth, she can't make a total commitment to David."

Darcy ate slowly, wanting to hear everything Constance had to say about the characters in the play. She hadn't realized that the teacher-student relationship was the heroine's real lifeline. The ending, a parting scene between Beth and David, had seemed tragic until she saw it through the eyes of the teacher. Beth would love again, but not until she was a complete person. Love as an escape was doomed to failure.

"I love the play," Darcy decided aloud, letting the tea grow cold as she listened with total absorption to Constance's ideas.

"Me too. I've never regretted leaving my college position to be part of it."

Talking to Constance didn't make Darcy an actress, but it did dispel some of her insecurity about the part. Working with the hearing-impaired, even in the relatively insignificant job as camp counselor, had taught her a lot she could apply to the role of Beth, if she could figure out how. At least she approached the morning rehearsal with a little less dread.

They practiced in the playhouse, this morning concentrating on Act I, beginning the session with the same stretching exercises Nick had done alone with her the night before. She was beginning to understand that body movement had a lot to do with acting; there had to be a gracefulness and sense of control in every action performed on the stage. Unfortunately, she still didn't know what to do with her hands and feet. Just being in the right spot at the right time demanded all her concentration.

Brett was having a terrible day. Cole Handley was riding him unmercifully whenever they were both out of a scene, and Darcy forgot her own worries as the man playing her father became more and more obnoxious.

"I've seen people kiss their parakeet with more feeling," Cole said, badgering the younger man when they took a ten-minute break for coffee.

Darcy noticed that the older actor's barbs were delivered quietly behind Nick's back, but Brett Dwyer's pride wouldn't allow him to complain to the director.

"He might do better if you'd be quiet," she said defensively, knowing she should stay out of their quarrel but hating a bully nonetheless.

"I thought we were going to have professional talent here

this summer," Cole said scornfully. "The Podunk Community Players can come up with stronger leads than you two."

Darcy knew she deserved his criticism, but Brett couldn't possibly be as bad as she was. "No one does well when they're harassed."

"Have I been harassing you?" Nick came up behind her just in time to hear her last statement.

"No, not you," she said quickly.

"I'm merely trying to give young Brett the benefit of my experience," Cole said in a patronizing voice.

"Let me do the directing, Cole," Nick said. "You've got your part down pat and so has Constance. Why don't the rest of you take the morning off, and I'll work alone with Sheila and Brett."

"If you think it will help," Cole said doubtfully.

"He is not a nice man," Darcy said half to herself as the older actor marched toward the exit.

Nick laughed softly. "Unfortunately, he's good."

"He's a bastard!" Brett said spitefully.

"Channel some of that antagonism into your feeling for Beth's father, and we'll have a play," Nick said, putting his hand on the young actor's shoulder to calm him.

They went through the park bench scene again and again and again, until Darcy thought she'd scream. How could Sheila stand the rehearsals, going over and over the same words and actions until they came automatically? Some actors stayed in the same play for years. No amount of audience enthusiasm would be reward enough for Darcy to endure such grueling repetition as a career.

"Much better," Nick said at last. "A little more polishing, and you'll have a great scene."

A little more rehearsing and she'd have sandpaper lips, Darcy thought. Brett didn't believe in stage kisses either. Just her luck to have a leading man with sour cigarette breath.

"Let's start again where David comes up behind you. This time, Sheila, don't cross your ankles."

She'd always known Sheila loved the applause and attention; she hadn't realized how hard her sister had to work for it. Either Nick was a slave driver, or actors labored like draft horses all the time. After a brief half-hour lunch break, Nick called the whole cast together again. Because their production time was fast approaching, he'd assigned the musical cast to the dining hall again this afternoon.

"I don't want to wear you out," he said, standing on the edge of the stage while the small cast sat in the seats, "so we'll go through the whole play once, then call it quits for today, except for Brett and Sheila. You two meet me in the lodge at seven thirty to work on the last scene."

The theater was hot, and Cole and Brett let their bickering color the whole rehearsal. Nick called them into his office afterward, and Sheila was grateful she wasn't getting his special attention this afternoon. The only pleasant things on her mind were a dip in the lake and a nap in the sun.

Her one-piece dark green bathing suit wasn't one Sheila would wear, but Darcy loved to swim without worrying about losing a flimsy bikini. She was the only one near the water, so she'd have to settle for a leisurely swim near the shoreline. Although she was a strong swimmer, she was still safety-conscious.

As she waded away from the beach, her feet sank into the sandy bottom covered with pebbles. The water temperature was much colder than she'd expected, but this far north the lake probably wouldn't feel warm until mid-summer. Plunging into waist-high ripples, she swam with a strong back-stroke, absorbing the sun's heat on her face.

The day had been a trial; even when Nick was silent and out of her range of vision, she was aware of him following her with his eyes, appraising her performance. He was wary of her, too, seldom addressing her directly, making quiet suggestions that seemed to include other cast members.

When she dared to look in his direction, his face had a puzzled frown.

Coming back to the shore, she walked up the narrow strip of beach that left sand sticking to her toes, toweling her hair as she went. She didn't see Nick until she nearly bumped into him.

"I didn't know you were such a good swimmer."

Sheila wasn't.

"It's relaxing," she said.

"About the only chance I get to enjoy the lake is early in the morning before everyone is up."

"You swim alone every morning?"

"Dangerous, I suppose, but no one seems interested in getting up at dawn to join me. Unless you are."

She'd love to swim with the sun just peeking over the eastern horizon at the end of the lake shaped like a duck's bill, but Sheila wouldn't dream of getting up that early.

"Of course, it's pretty chilly then," Nick added.

"I need exercise." She tried not to show how much she'd like to join him.

"You look fit to me. I've never seen you looking better."

"Thank you."

"You could try it once. If it's too early or too cold, you can forget it."

"What time do you swim?"

"I set my alarm for six. Mrs. Corning is just putting the coffee on."

"I suppose once wouldn't hurt." Maybe she did have potential as an actress. Disguising her eagerness took some talent!

"Good. I'll knock on your door to make sure you don't change your mind."

"I'll be ready."

The evening rehearsal didn't go well. Brett was inconsistent, doing extremely well in a scene then folding the next time they tried it. Darcy recognized in him some of the same

54

traits she found in children with speech problems: insecurity and fear of ridicule. Brett did best when he was continually reassured. Nick's whole approach to directing was to build confidence and help the actors develop their characters, but Brett needed an extra boost. Much to her surprise, Darcy found herself supplying it. She was the last person to give anyone acting lessons, but all her co-star needed was encouragement. Working under Nick's constant scrutiny, it took a lot out of her to supply it.

After the evening rehearsal she tried on some dresses for Fran, the costume head, and between them they worked out her wardrobe for every scene, although Darcy wasn't completely happy with all the selections. Fran chose pastels with emphasis on pale, deep shades to emphasize Beth's youth, innocence, and withdrawal from the world. She listened to Darcy's reasoning that the deaf girl would wear jeans to the park like any other young woman. Darcy was sure Beth, hungering for the real world, would try to look as normal and ordinary as possible. After some discussion, Fran vetoed wearing jeans, insisting that some of the mood would be lost. All the costumes seemed a little matronly to Darcy, but she didn't want to argue.

Nick worked late, too, staying in the theater to help test some lights with the technician. Darcy heard his voice as she left but didn't see him.

As soon as she dropped onto the bed, she was asleep, blanking out like an overloaded circuit but waking up before her alarm rang in the morning. Surprisingly, she felt marvelous, relaxed and energetic, ready to face whatever demands the day brought. Working on a play was so stimulating, she almost envied her sister, but her practical nature ruled out that career for herself. She'd hate to live the way Sheila did, always struggling for recognition and scampering for parts, never sure from one season to the next whether she'd be working. In the gentle light of early dawn, Darcy felt nothing but sympathy for her sister, driven by ambitions that were hard to fulfill.

Her swimsuit, hanging to dry on the shower rod, was damp in the seams and crotch, making it feel icy on her skin. Shivering, she wrapped the largest available towel around her shoulders and wondered if Nick would remember to come for her. He did, knocking softly only moments after she put on the suit.

"Good morning. I can't believe you're ready to swim." He smiled, closing the door when she walked out ahead of him.

"I'm looking forward to it."

Sheila would say something clever or witty and fish for compliments, but Darcy didn't feel like playing the role of her sister. She wanted to be herself and enjoy being with the attractive man escorting her to the lake.

Nick's swimming briefs were dark navy jersey with a single gold stripe on either side, riding up on his buttocks as he walked. He twisted and swung a towel in the air, curiously boyish, fidgeting and saying nothing. Barefooted, she lagged behind, gingerly watching where she stepped when she wasn't distracted by the figure just ahead of her. Nick reached the lakeside strip of sand, tossing his towel on the ground and waiting for her to do the same.

"Are you cold?" he asked.

"It is a little chilly." She wasn't sure her shivering had anything to do with the temperature.

He put his arm around her shoulders, pulling her close as they advanced toward the water.

"I'm really surprised that you're doing this. Is it because you want to be with me?"

How could she answer that question? She didn't try, and he didn't press her.

A pebble caught between her toes as they waded hand in hand into deeper water. Lifting her foot, she bent to dislodge it, giggling when a small fish startled her by flicking against her calf.

Nick dove, pulling her under with him, and laughed when she came up sputtering.

"Quick is best," he teased.

"I like to go in slowly!" She ran fingers over her eyes to clear them of water. "I'll race you to the end of the lake." She pointed at a yellow boat house at the far point of the duck's bill.

"It's farther than it looks," he warned.

"You're not up to it?"

"Lead off!" He accepted her challenge with a pleased grin.

He gave her a long head start, and she didn't like it, treading water and calling back for him to get going. As soon as he started slicing through the water with a powerful crawl, she knew why he'd waited. He was fast, much too powerful for her to outdistance, but she gave the race her best effort, pacing herself and concentrating on the finish. Even working her hardest, she knew he could beat her without any strain.

Instead of gloating over his easy victory, he was lavish in his praise.

"I had no idea you could swim so well."

"No charity!" She pulled herself out of the water onto the dock beside the yellow boat house. "You could beat me with your feet tied together."

"I swam on the team in college, remember?"

How could she remember what she'd never known? Sitting beside him on the edge of the plank dock, she dangled her feet in the water beside his, averting her eyes because the sight of his strong legs with wet hair matted against tanned skin was uncomfortably appealing. Wringing water from her hair, she tried not to see the swell of muscle on his arm, beaded with droplets of water, or the expanse of his thigh so close to hers. Swimming together was a way of getting acquainted fast, but she'd been foolish to come. The more time she spent with Nick, the less she understood how her sister could have left him.

"Why did you leave me, Sheila?"

57

His question so closely reflected her own thoughts that she wanted to melt between the boards and disappear in the dark water under the dock.

"I don't know." It was the only honest answer she could give, but her deceitfulness in pretending to be Sheila filled her with self-loathing.

She was desperately trying to think of a way to tell him the truth when his arm encircled her shoulders and he gently kissed the hollow of her neck.

"For a while," he said, drawing her closer, "I hated you, then I decided I was better off without you. All I felt when I learned you'd be here was indifference. I was over you, Sheila, good-bye and good riddance. What are you doing to me now?"

"You didn't feel anything anymore?" She forced the question through her constricted throat.

"Not a damn thing! I almost believe you're practicing witchcraft, brewing potions so I'll be wild about you again."

"Don't say that! Please, Nick, don't feel that way! I'll only be here until the play is over, then we may never see each other again. I don't want you to be hurt when I leave."

"You don't want me to be hurt?" He sounded stunned. "You've been saying some strange things since you got here, but I can't believe I'm hearing that from you." He put his hands on both sides of her face, forcing her to look at him, but she couldn't meet his eyes. "Maybe you are becoming a real actress. I almost think you're sincere."

"We'd better go back," she said weakly.

"No, not until I check out the new Sheila a little more."

He kissed her more slowly, pulling her into his arms until she was crushed against the water-cooled skin of his chest. Extraordinary sensations made her part her lips, hungry for the taste and touch of him, and the skin around her mouth tingled. Sinking backward, hands clutching at his firm shoulders, she felt smooth, hard boards under her back. Trapped but unresisting, she kept her eyes closed as his lips explored her face.

"Whose dock is this?" she managed to murmur when he halted his kisses and hovered over her, a look of expectancy on his face.

"Whose dock?" He was genuinely puzzled. "When did you start worrying about propriety?"

"I'm going back." She tried to squirm free but couldn't get away until he released her.

"Sheila." There was exasperation, frustration, and something else in his tone. "Why now? Why leave me and then let things start up between us again?"

"Nothing's starting!" she denied, feeling defeated and disappointed because she couldn't let anything start up between the two of them.

"No?" He kissed her again, savage in his determination to get a response.

She didn't want to feel the way she did. It was horrible to take her sister's place in another man's arms, especially when he thought it was Sheila writhing under him beside the quiet lake. Emphatically pushing him away, she felt as if his kisses were imprinted on her skin, guilty reminders that she was behaving deceitfully.

"I'm going back." She dropped into the water and swam toward the playhouse with more urgency and determination than she'd had racing Nick.

Unable to outdistance him, she was aware of his wake to her left as he paced her to within a few hundred yards of the beach where they'd started.

"Sheila!"

When she didn't stop, he sprinted ahead, catching her in his arms.

"We'll talk more tonight," he said.

"No." Her breathlessness had nothing to do with swimming.

"I'll come to your cabin when I'm done."

"No, don't."

"Just to talk." He wasn't paying any attention to her no's.

Leaving her, he gained the beach fifty yards ahead of her and walked rapidly to his towel. After shaking out the sand he toweled his head, keeping his back toward Darcy, who was just emerging from the water.

Watching him with his legs spread apart and water glistening on well-developed shoulders, she felt a tightness in her throat that threatened to bring tears. Sheila used and discarded men like soiled tissues; she always had, and Nick probably meant nothing at all to her right now. Once in high school Darcy had had a terrible crush on Jake, one of Sheila's admirers. When her twin got a date with a college man over Christmas break, she'd persuaded Darcy to take her place on a date with Jake. Infatuated with the handsome football player, Darcy confessed the truth to him, hoping he'd like her for herself. Instead he'd been furiously angry at Sheila who, in her turn, was enraged at Darcy. Jake forgave her sister within a week but never stopped showing his disdain for Darcy.

She hoped what she was feeling for Nick was only infatuation. Nothing good could happen if she started falling in love with one of Sheila's men.

All day Nick was polite but remote; his kisses on the dock might never have happened. If anything, he seemed to regret his own weakness, taking elaborate care not to show any special interest in her. At first it was a relief when he didn't talk to her, but by afternoon she was willing to settle for any small scrap of attention he'd give her.

"Are you angry with me?" she finally dared ask when they were alone for a moment after the afternoon rehearsal.

"No, not angry." He sounded weary. "Maybe you really have changed, Sheila. I'm just not sure I want to care for you again."

"I don't blame you."

"No? You keep surprising me. Once you'd have blamed

me if you blew an audition or had a disagreement with your agent. Is this a new game you're playing?"

"I'm not playing. I'm sorry I said anything. Just forget it."

"Not likely. We'll talk about it in your cabin tonight."

"No!"

"You owe me a few minutes of honest conversation. You're doing a mediocre job in the play, and I've been too easy on you. We can talk in my office or your cabin, but I think the cabin would be more private." He nodded at an apprentice hurrying past with an awkwardly heavy wooden bannister, a prop in Act II.

She wasn't experienced enough to know how she was doing in the play. Since talking to Constance, she understood her character better, but there were so many techniques of stagecraft that she hadn't mastered. In the eyes of an expert like Nick, she had to be blowing it badly.

"My cabin, then," she said morosely. She didn't want anyone else to hear what he had to say about her meager acting ability. "Only to talk about the play."

"I don't think we can talk about your part without discussing our relationship. For some reason, I'm making you awfully nervous."

He was certainly right about that, she thought.

No one complained about Mrs. Corning's meals, except perhaps those who wished they weren't so tempting and fattening. Dinner was usually a pleasant interlude when cast and crew talked over their mutual concerns and interests. Tonight was the exception.

During both the morning and afternoon rehearsals, Cole had ignored Brett, but at dinner he began baiting the younger actor again.

"Well, boy wonder," Cole said setting his tray down across from Brett, "I hear your father's all washed up on that soap opera of his."

"It's none of your business," Brett snapped. "You're still

61

jealous because you didn't get the part yourself twelve years ago."

"Me play Dr. Sudsy Woebegone? I did a TV movie that year."

"Sure, two walk-ons in a rehash of a Hollywood rehash. That's why you're on my case all the time, isn't it? My dad beat you out of the soap part, and you're having fun sticking it to me. Well, I'm getting damn sick of it!"

"Brett, let's talk this over later," Nick said in a low, warning voice.

"Talk! That's all the old bastard can do! It's like squeezing a garbage bag and all the trash squirts out." The young actor rose, angrily knocking his chair to the floor behind him.

"I don't have to take this," Cole said, and muttered a string of obscenities as he stood up.

"Both of you, cool down!" Nick ordered, stepping up to Brett and taking his arm in a steely grasp.

"I wouldn't have come here if I'd known that old has-been would be lousing up the summer."

"You're not professional enough to be on the same stage with a real actor," Cole said with biting sarcasm.

"Professional! You're a professional know-it-all!" Brett was red in the face, clutching his fists and obviously wanting to hit the older man.

"Come on," Nick ordered curtly. "We'll have this out in my office." He ushered the two antagonists out of the dining hall.

The room was absolutely silent for a moment, then conversation began as a low buzz, building in volume as the others speculated about the bad feelings between the two men.

"Nick will have to be another Solomon to work things out between those two," Constance said. "The play is suffering too much to let it go on. I know the tension must be affecting your part, too, Sheila."

The quarrel between Brett and Cole had nothing to do

with Darcy's performance, but she wasn't in any position to confess that to the woman who'd been so friendly to her.

"I guess bad feelings in the cast bother everyone's acting, but I don't see how yours could be improved."

"Thank you," Constance said, smiling warmly. "I just hope Nick has a miracle up his sleeve."

The blowup wasn't enough to make her forget that Nick was coming to her cabin. Since first meeting him, Darcy had tried to remember some fragment of information Sheila might have dropped about their relationship. In infrequent phone calls, her sister tossed off tidbits of information, but she'd never mentioned Nicholas Cross. Darcy was sure she hadn't.

There was only one person who might know where Sheila was staying: her agent, Manfred Zwarles. His name was unusual; even in New York City there couldn't be too many Manfred Zwarles in the telephone directory.

Nick's office door was shut when she went to the theater; he might still be closeted with the two quarrelsome actors. As usual the box office was locked, and not until after nine o'clock was the kitchen completely deserted. Darcy crept in there feeling sly and sneaky, managing to reach directory assistance for Manhattan. As she hoped, the phone book wasn't overloaded with a name like Manfred Zwarles. Unfortunately, his home phone was unlisted. She wrote down the number of his agency in case she had a chance to call him in the morning. Even if he could tell her where Sheila was, knowing tomorrow wasn't going to help her tonight. Nick was coming to her cabin.

She went back to the little room to wait for him, sitting in the only chair, comfortable enough with plastic cushions and wooden arms, and holding a book on her lap, not even pretending to read. The wait turned out to be a long one.

CHAPTER FOUR

A soft knock roused her, but she was slow in uncoiling from a cramped position in the old chair. The plastic cushion stuck to bare thighs when she tried to stand, and her neck was stiff. The paperback she'd been holding was on the floor, and her left arm was marked by a deep red ridge from the wooden armrest.

"Coming," she called, trying to straighten her wrinkled shorts and clinging knit top.

"I know it's late, but I saw your light," Nick said.

"I fell asleep in the chair. How late is it?"

"After midnight. Sorry I woke you. I thought you might be waiting up for me." He stepped inside and shut the door. "They should put screen doors on these cabins."

"I guess summer theaters operate on tight budgets."

Now that he was here, he seemed to fill the small bedroom. Fatigue made him look more rugged than usual, and a thin white scar by the corner of his mouth added a hint of menace to his drawn face.

"Duckeye pays guest players well, I think. Isn't that the reason you're here?"

"My agent thought coming here would be good for me." At least she knew this much about her sister's career. "I didn't know you'd be here," she told him again.

"No, I'm sure you didn't." He sat on the edge of her bed and took off his shoes, stretching out lazily with both pillows under his head and shoulders.

"Make yourself comfortable," she said a bit sarcastically.

"It's been a long day. Lie beside me, and we'll talk." He shifted his hips into a more comfortable indentation on the lumpy mattress.

"I can talk from here." She pushed the chair farther from the bed and sat down on the edge so her legs wouldn't stick to the plastic again. "You have the wrong—"

"Idea?" he interrupted.

What he really had was the wrong sister, and Darcy didn't know what he'd expect from Sheila.

"You said you wanted to talk." She crossed her arms over her breasts, a gesture of withdrawal that he didn't miss.

"I want to know what your game is."

"There's no game," she answered with a puzzled frown.

"It's sheer coincidence that you're treating me so nicely, giving me encouragement, maybe even leading me on?"

"You're exaggerating!" She hoped he was; it was devastating to think her interest was so obvious.

"Drop it, Sheila," he said wearily. "We didn't exactly part on friendly terms."

"That was a long time ago."

"Was it?" He might look relaxed, but his voice had a razor-sharp edge.

"Nick, there's something I have to tell you."

She'd fallen asleep wearing sandals, and one strap was cutting into the top of her foot, making it itch. Bending to loosen her shoes, she tried to think of some way to tell Nick the truth without ruining Sheila's reputation and career.

"I'm listening."

"I can't tell you unless you promise not to be angry, not to do anything to get even."

He laughed harshly. "Blind promises, sweetheart? Not a chance!"

"You resent me. You don't want me here," she said slowly, reacting to the message in his eyes.

"Of course I resent what you're doing to me! You can't

think I want to be in love with you again!" He sprang up and stood over her, diminishing her courage with his words and closeness.

"You're making a mistake—"

"Don't I know it!"

"I'm not—"

"I know exactly what you are!"

"Nick!" She tried to stand and put distance between them, but he wouldn't let her evade him.

She wanted to be in his arms; that was the terrible part.

"You are so wicked," he murmured just before his mouth covered hers.

"You said you wanted to talk," she gasped, trying to struggle away from his hungry, aggressive kisses.

"When have we ever solved anything by talking?" he asked, effectively taking her prisoner within the circle of his arms.

"You don't understand!"

His answer was a hard kiss delivered with an exaggerated smacking sound. He was tormenting her, not making love, and her temper flared. Let Nick think she was Sheila! Darcy didn't deserve his high-handed treatment, and he didn't deserve to know the truth!

"Come here," he said, half dragging and half carrying her to the bed. "We do talk the same language in bed."

"No!" She pushed against his chest with both hands as he hovered over her.

"What's wrong?" His voice was low and seductive as he slid his hand under her knit top, caressing the swell of breast under her bra.

Everything was wrong, and, worst of all, his gentle touch was wonderful, stroking away her will to resist. When he kissed her again, she parted her lips, letting his tongue pass the ivory ridge of teeth and explore the moistness of her mouth. Moaning when he withdrew, she buried her fingers in the thick mahogany hair on the back of his head and shivered as his hands grew bolder.

He inched up her shirt and loosened her bra, pushing it out of the way and cupping both breasts in his hands, paying homage to first one and then the other with his lips.

"Your breasts are blushing," he said with wonderment. "I don't remember such a rosy tint on your nipples." He kissed each one slowly, making heat rush to her cheeks and fire ignite between her thighs.

He couldn't remember the pinkness of her nipples because Sheila's were much darker. Nick was making love to her sister, *not her,* and, as aroused as she was, she suddenly found it intolerable to be a stand-in lover.

"Nick, I don't want this," she said hoarsely, pushing away his hands.

"I don't believe you." He slid one hand between her thighs, maddening her with little squeezes.

"Please don't!"

Intent on exploring the silkiness of her skin with his fingers, he paid no heed to her protests until she started struggling to evade him.

"I don't understand." He sat upright, looking more confused than angry. "I know you too well to misread the signals you've been sending."

He didn't know her at all! "I just want you to leave, Nick, please."

"You've never been a tease. Why start now, Sheila?"

His hand on her stomach felt as heavy as a brick.

Groping for the right words and trying to ignore the hurt in his voice, she could only stammer, "Please, don't."

"All right, but tell me why." He rested his hands, palms up, on his own thighs.

"I'm just not in the mood!"

His laugh hurt more than a slap. "That's the corniest line you've ever delivered."

"There's no reason why you should think I'm available just because I'm here!"

"That's the last thing I think! Do you have any idea how many miserable, sleepless nights I had after you left?"

She shook her head, numb with misery.

"I'm not surprised," he said bitterly. "I just don't understand. Why swim with me? Why make me think there might still be something between us?"

"I don't know!"

"That's a stupid answer, Sheila! You must know how you feel about me, or what you want from me."

"No." She shook her head, trying to summon forth a lie that would send him away.

She wasn't an actress; it was impossible to say he meant nothing to her. In order to tell him the whole truth, she'd have to admit she was falling in love with him. Instead she averted her head, squeezing her eyes shut so he couldn't read her frustrated longing.

"Something's wrong," he said dejectedly. "One way or another I'm going to find out what."

"Please leave," she begged, holding back tears with Amazonian effort.

"I had another reason for coming here tonight," he said woodenly. "The play. Why are you holding back so much with your part? Is it because I'm directing?"

"No." She averted her face, feeling one hot tear escape from under her right eyelid and run a zigzag course down her cheek. "Can't we talk about it tomorrow?"

"Why not now?"

Too sharp-eyed for her comfort, he touched the damp spot on her cheek with his thumb. "Tears, Sheila? You can turn them on as well as anyone in the business, but why pretend to cry now?"

"I'm not pretending!" Grabbing a pillow to cover her exposed breasts, she slid off the bed and retreated as far as possible in the tiny room, clutching the down-filled shield in front of her.

"I made a mistake coming to your cabin," he said. "I'm sorry."

"It was my fault. I didn't realize, I didn't know . . ."

"Are you admitting you could be guilty of something? Sheila, you astonish me. Where's the selfish little schemer I thought I loved?"

Darcy was dying to say "She's in California," but her throat was too constricted to speak. She heard rather than saw Nick putting on his shoes and leaving, banging the door behind him with an echo of finality.

Turning the bolt to secure the door for the night, she pressed her forehead against the hard wooden frame and let bottled-up tears spill down her face. Her shoulders shook as noisy sobs racked her body, and she used the pillow to muffle the sounds of her misery. If she didn't love Nick, she could tell him the truth. What she couldn't handle was his scorn and contempt, her just punishment for agreeing to her sister's hoax. She hated herself for going along with the deception, so how could Nick do anything but despise her? This was much, much worse than the fiasco with Jake in high school. She wasn't an infatuated teenager, sure to find another love interest in a few weeks or months. The pain of loving Nick was going to last a long, long time.

Still emotionally exhausted when she awoke in the morning, Darcy at least felt more rational. How could she possibly be in love with Nicholas Cross after knowing him such a short time? Maybe she was childishly competing with her twin, wanting to share in Sheila's romantic adventures with men. The only thing to do, she decided, was forget Nick.

More than ever she wanted to talk to Sheila, if only to vent some of her anger at her sister for getting her into an impossible situation. The first chance she had, she'd try contacting Manfred Zwarles again.

Standing under the gentle spray of a warm shower, Darcy

let the water pelt her head and shoulders then run in rivulets down her back. She'd never felt more aware of her body. No one had ever caressed her breasts with Nick's gentle sensitivity; remembering his touch made her nipples harden and her body ache with desire. If he were beside her now . . .

Furious at herself for conjuring up erotic fantasies about her sister's ex-lover, she stepped out of the shower stall and vigorously dried herself on one of the coarse towels furnished with the cabin. Sick of playing the part of Sheila, she pulled on serviceable cotton underpants over her tingling legs and hips, then brushed her wet hair into a tight twist secured on top of her head with the clips Nick didn't like. Sandals, bra, slacks, and a neat, tailored, white oxford cloth blouse, long sleeves rolled to her elbows, completed her outfit for the day. She knew she was stuck in this horrible charade, but from now on she was determined to play it her way.

Selecting a breakfast that was anything but exotic—oatmeal, orange juice, and whole wheat toast with honey—she walked past the table where Nick was sitting with Ken and several of the stage manager's apprentices. She nodded stiffly when he looked up at her and sat beside Constance, greeting her with forced cheerfulness.

"Well, what do you think of your new leading man?" Constance asked, arching her pencil-thin brows.

"Isn't Brett going to be in the play?"

"No, he's in the chorus of *Carousel* instead. Nick had to do some clever rearranging to make everyone happy. I guess Brett will get his chance at a lead in August."

"Nick took him out of the play just because Cole doesn't like him?"

"No, Brett wanted out. Cole likes to have someone around to heckle, but he won't get anywhere with the new David."

"Who is he?" Darcy didn't really care, but Constance's secret amusement was annoying.

"Nick."

"Nick is taking the part? He can't! He's the director!"

"It's not impossible to act and direct with such a small cast. Everyone but the apprentices has done *Wings of Love* before this."

"But we open next week!"

"Nick will know the part. Don't look so worried."

Constance was too kind to say "Why not worry about your own part a little more," but Darcy could see the unspoken rebuke on her friend's face.

The oatmeal went down like flour paste, and Darcy abandoned the rest of her breakfast as soon as Constance left to write a few letters before morning rehearsal. Playing romantic scenes with Nick would be unbearable, she thought. Somehow she had to contact her sister and tell her the switch was over. Forgetting to worry about being overheard, she made a credit card call on the kitchen phone, reaching the agent's office but not getting through to Zwarles himself. There was no way she could leave a number for him to call; in fact, Mrs. Corning was paying too much attention to her conversation with the agent's secretary. She'd have to call later from a more private location.

She nearly bumped into Nick as she pushed through the swinging door between the kitchen and dining hall.

"Why didn't you tell me you were taking Brett's place?" she asked, her lips pale with anger.

"The subject didn't come up. Come with me, would you please?" He put his hand on her arm.

"I'd rather not be alone with you," she said unhappily.

"Sheila—no, damn it, I'm not going to apologize! What I have to say is professional, not personal. Let's go down to the lake."

Sure that he was going to talk about the poor job she was doing in the play, Darcy followed him with bitter reluctance. She wasn't used to failure; in her real career as a speech pathologist, she enjoyed the approval of her co-workers and

71

the satisfaction of knowing she was involved in an important profession. She gave children self-confidence as well as a better command of vowels and consonants, showing a loving concern for all her cases. Here she didn't know as much as the greenest apprentice; if the part weren't a silent one, she would have been fired by now.

"Through the trees here," Nick said, catching her hand in his.

Pulling her hand away would make an issue of his casual gesture. She submitted to his touch to avoid a scene, or so she tried to believe.

He sat on the ground with his back against the rough blackish bark of a tree trunk, spreading his legs wide then restlessly pulling up his knees. Darcy looked at the lake, hazy bluish-green beyond the band of shallow water near shore, then studied a cluster of little purple violets growing wild in the sparse growth of grass close to the beach. Stooping, she picked a single tiny bloom, saving it from the cutting blades an apprentice would push over it later in the day, sniffing it and discovering no detectable fragrance as her nostrils inhaled the clean, damp lakeside air. Unwilling to discard the fragile blossom, she tucked it into the second of the two buttonholes she'd left open.

"Your sign language is much more believable than I'd expected," Nick began slowly, pulling at a blade of grass and examining it on his palm as if it were the first he'd seen. "And you do know the part; you never miss a cue."

His tact was making her more uncomfortable than the harshness she expected and thought she deserved.

"I've been blaming myself," he said, flicking away the grass and stretching his legs far enough to sink the heels of his rubber-soled moccasins into the sand of the beach. "I wish you'd sit."

She did, keeping a yard between them, squatting on her heels.

"If something else is making you so tense, tell me. I'll try

72

to understand. I don't believe you want this play to be a flop any more than I do."

"No, I don't," she said truthfully, wishing she did have enough talent to make Beth come alive.

"That, at least, is one thing we have in common," he said dryly.

She stared at his arm, the dark hairs on golden-tan skin. The knit cuff of his golf shirt hugged his upper arm, soft white material against the taut swell of muscle. She wanted to cup his elbow in her palm and feel the beat of his pulse at his wrist. His fingers were long and slender with prominent knuckles and clean, short nails. Remembering how his hand had covered her breast, she longed to hug it to her cheek, press little kisses against the warm skin.

". . . give it all our spare time," he was saying.

"I'm sorry. I wasn't listening," she said contritely.

"What were you thinking?"

"Oh, nothing."

"Tell me one thing," he said slowly. "Is there someone else?"

"No!" She spoke before thinking, then remembered her sister's interest in Tony Adler.

Nick sighed deeply and stood, offering her his hand. She let him pull her to her feet, not sorry when he held her fingers in his for a long, silent moment.

"I wish I could believe you," he said guardedly. "Did you hear what I said about the two of us working the stiffness out of your part?"

She shook her head, embarrassed by her inattentiveness.

"We'll get together this evening. The kitchen is probably the only large room not in use then. Meet me there at eight. I'll see you at morning rehearsal in a few minutes."

She let herself feast on the sight of his retreating figure, loving the square set of his shoulders and the way his hair hugged the back of his neck. His spine was erect without being rigid, and his buns were delightful, round and hard.

Studying his physical beauty lightened her spirit. It was natural to be physically attracted to a well-built, handsome man, she thought. Probably most of the young women serving as apprentices had mad crushes on him. Just because she was a few years older didn't mean she wasn't susceptible to his masculine charm. Imagining that she was in love was foolish. Love had to grow slowly out of mutual interests and values. She absolutely had to stop confusing attraction with love, she told herself.

The day's rehearsals were grueling. Familiar as he was with the play, Nick was quick at memorizing the lines, but still not letter-perfect. Even Cole went out of his way to be cooperative, but fatigue was starting to tell before they quit for dinner. Constance organized a small excursion to go into Traverse City for a movie, but the majority of the playhouse cast and crew, including Darcy, had more work to do in the evening. She envied the small, carefree group that set off for some badly needed recreation.

The *Carousel* dancers were using the dining hall, practicing to the somewhat tinny music of the number two piano. On stage in the theater the two leads in the musical were working on their scenes together. Darcy thought the second show of the season was in better shape to open than *Wings of Love.*

"Good, you're on time," Nick said when he found her in the kitchen.

Once again Darcy was reminded of how different she and her twin were. Sheila was always late. With a surge of irritation, she wondered why Nick couldn't see for himself that she wasn't her sister. He seemed to know everything there was to know about Sheila; why didn't he realize that Darcy couldn't possibly be the woman he'd known intimately in the past?

"You did better in the scene with your father today," Nick said.

74

Was she imagining things, or was there a trace of nervousness in his voice?

"Thank you."

It had been easy to act hostile to Cole. She was furious at him for driving Brett out of the play.

"Let's begin with the park bench scene," Nick said. "I think I have the lines now."

"You're a fast study."

"By the time a play opens, I know most of the lines just from hearing them so often. Here, use this stool as the park bench. It's a little high but it'll do."

She sat down on a backless metal stool used by Mrs. Corning when she needed to rest her feet. With Nick behind her she remembered how she'd studied him that morning when he walked away from the beach. Was he doing the same to her right now? she wondered.

"Relax!" he ordered, but it was a command that produced the opposite effect.

"You leave me no choice," he said softly, coming up behind her and kneading her shoulders with hard fingers.

There was nothing erotic about this massage. He worked on her tense muscles until they were pliant and relaxed, using only slightly less pressure when she said "ouch" several times. Moving to her neck, he was more gentle but no less persistent, insisting that her head loll on her neck before he stopped.

"I know if you're too rigid now, it's in your head," he said, directing the winning force of his smile at her for the first time that day.

Nothing she'd tried on stage had worked well, but tonight Darcy pretended she was Beth, concentrating so hard on the thoughts the deaf girl might be thinking that she was genuinely startled when Nick came up behind her, beginning the scene.

In their earlier rehearsals together, he'd lightly touched her shoulders and simulated the kiss by pressing his mouth against her chin. Nothing like that happened tonight. His hands slid downward until his fingers rested lightly on her nipples, creating a sensation like a faint electrical charge. Because, at this moment, she was Beth eagerly hoping to see the man she loved, Darcy accepted his caress as natural and pleasing, turning with joy to welcome him into her arms.

The audience wouldn't see a stage kiss if Nick covered her mouth with his during the performance as he did now, extracting its sweetness with persistence and ardor. If Darcy's part had been a speaking one, she wouldn't have had enough breath to utter a word.

When they finished the scene, Darcy really did feel relaxed.

"Much better," Nick said. "You see, there's still something good left between us."

"The play is a separate thing," she said without believing it herself. Beth had been warm and loving with David in the scene because that's the way Darcy wanted to be with Nick.

They went through less important scenes, coming at last to the closing scene, where Beth said good-bye to David. To be successful, Constance had explained at a rehearsal, the scene had to leave the audience with hope; people had to believe that the young lovers would find happiness, together or separately, even though they weren't ready to make a lifetime commitment.

Darcy thought about never seeing Nick again, and the emotional parting in the play became much more realistic. Without conscious effort, her carriage and gestures mirrored the sorrow of the deaf woman who had to put love aside until she found herself. Darcy was trembling in Nick's arms when they came together for a final embrace.

"You were great!" He lightly kissed her forehead and beamed his approval. "I'd like to take credit, but it has to be more than a massage that made you come alive the way you just did."

"Thank you."

76

His praise was embarrassing because she didn't deserve it; all she'd done was use the way she felt about Nick to play the part.

He stood beside her for a moment, resting his hand lightly on the back of her waist, pricking her conscience because his kindness was so undeserved. She couldn't go on deceiving herself as well as him. What she felt was no schoolgirl crush or biological urge. This man could easily become the center of her universe.

The rehearsal was over; there was nothing more to do that evening, but neither made any move to leave, pretending interest in their surroundings. The kitchen had a faint odor from the restaurant-size gas range, even with the windows open. The water and coffee had already been measured and placed in a big stainless steel coffee maker for the next day's breakfast, and twin white bakery boxes of doughnuts were sitting on a well-scrubbed Formica counter. One end of the room was dominated by a huge glass-doored cooler, pad-locked in Mrs. Corning's absence.

"Are you hungry?" Nick asked.

She nodded. "Thirsty too."

"Mrs. Corning doesn't trust actors in her fridge. Do you want a doughnut?"

"Not really."

"Let's go out for something. Beer and pizza? No, you don't like beer. I have a better idea."

They were nearly out of the now-empty lodge before the phone rang. Nick heard it and raced back with Darcy following him to the door of the kitchen, holding it open against her shoulder while he answered it.

"It's for you," he said, handing her the receiver and looking slightly puzzled.

"Hello."

"Darcy, who was that?" Sheila asked.

"The director." Darcy spoke softly and glanced at Nick,

77

wishing he'd leave so she could say what needed to be said to her sister.

"Not Julius?" Sheila pressed for an identification.

"No, Nicholas Cross."

"Oh, dear!"

"Yes, a big surprise," Darcy said emphatically. "Where are you?"

"We're staying with a friend of Tony's in Beverly Hills. I've met some fabulous people and—"

"Give me your number," Darcy interrupted, clutching a pencil Mrs. Corning had tied to a cork board on a piece of twine.

Scribbling down the phone number, Darcy had to bite her lower lip to keep from screaming at her sister. "Will you be there tomorrow?" she asked urgently.

"Maybe we'll have dinner here. I'm dying to know what Nick is doing at the Duckeye. Is he still furious with me? How are you handling him? Are you two alone together now?"

How could her sister bombard her with questions? Sheila was the one who should be supplying the answers.

"I'll call you tomorrow," Darcy said, hanging up in irritation. "My sister can be a pest," she said to Nick, tucking the number in her jean's pocket and hurrying out of the kitchen.

"You've never told me much about her," Nick said.

"Oh, she grew up in pokey old Springfield, just like me," Darcy said, giving her best imitation of Sheila. "Same parents and all that." If Nick didn't know they were twins, this certainly wasn't the time to tell him.

"Your voices sound a lot alike."

"Yes, people often mistake us on the phone."

"You didn't talk long. Sorry if I should've left."

"Oh, no, we don't have all that much to say. She's on vacation. I just wanted her number in case of emergency."

"My car's down here," he said taking her arm. "What does your sister do?"

Why did he want to know about her sister? Darcy tried to think of some way to change the subject.

"She's a speech pathologist. I should run to the cabin for my purse."

"You won't need it. My treat."

"My hair—"

"I don't mind it this way." He stopped and fingered a single strand that had fallen free over one ear.

His car was the dark blue BMW parked at the far end of the lodge, which told her he obviously didn't make his living in summer stock, but Darcy didn't know how to ask about his career without betraying her ignorance. Sheila was going to get a phone call a lot sooner than she expected.

"What will you do after you leave here?" she asked as they drove along a dark, tree-flanked country road.

"I'll only be here until August fifteenth. Then I have to get started on a new play in New York. This is supposed to be my vacation."

Hers too, she remembered.

Old Vienna was a new roadhouse—a combination restaurant, bar, and dance hall that seemed to appeal to young locals as well as summer people. There was a lively crowd and a terrible band that played a combination of country and rock that sounded like a demolition team tearing apart a train engine. She and Nick were shown to a table beside a varnished log wall by a waitress in a thigh-length yellow sweater-dress and spike heels that made Darcy realize there were tougher jobs than pretending to be an actress.

A woman at the next table was wearing a green strapless satin dress, and at the bar a motorcycle gang still wearing their leather jackets was downing pitchers of beer. It was the kind of place where no one under forty feels out of place. Nick grinned at the silliness of being there, and she wondered how close her estimate of his age was; he looked thirty when he smiled and thirty-five when he frowned.

They ordered a liter of Margaritas, followed by Reuben

sandwiches so smothered in Swiss cheese and kraut they had to eat them with forks. Darcy relaxed because it was far too noisy for conversation; she could barely hear Nick's comments and questions, and he accepted a smile as her answer to everything he said.

She didn't want to dance because Sheila had inherited all the grace and rhythm in the family, but Nick insisted, steering her toward a polished wooden floor about the size of a pool table and so crowded that bumping rumps seemed to be as much a part of the action as wild gyrations. The band had a primitive beat that created an everything- goes free-for-all, and she followed Nick's lead, grinning back at him because they both knew it was silly but fun. They left the floor laughing.

"Crazy place!" she said when they were out in the graveled parking area. "How did you find it?"

"One of the techs took me before you came." He pulled her close with one arm around her shoulders, not releasing her when they reached the car.

"One for the road," he said lightly, bending to kiss her.

It was a warm kiss that manipulated her mouth in a fantastic way, as primitive as the music that drifted out to the tree-bordered parking lot and as passionate as the blood pounding in her ears. The rough stones underfoot crunched as they pressed closer, and Nick none too gently yanked out the clips that held her tight twist, burying his face in the wild raven strands of newly liberated hair.

Wherever they touched there was heat, hot searing passion that defied the pleasantly cool night air which swept over the breadth of Lake Michigan. Straining on tiptoes to feel the bones of his jaw and cheeks pressed against hers, she writhed as his fingers traveled over her buttocks, squeezing and kneading until the contours of their bodies were like interlocking pieces of a jigsaw puzzle.

A few hundred feet away a noisy crowd piled into a van and drove away, bringing them back to the actual time and place. He opened the car door for her with one hand, kissing her even more intensely before letting her collapse on the seat.

They drove back to Mallard Lake in silence, making contact only when he rested his hand on her thigh, driving that way for a short distance then returning his hand to the wheel.

If he tried to make love to her, she'd tell him the truth. Anything else was unthinkable.

The access road was deserted; not a single car passed them after they left the highway. Nick drove past the theater and parked his car in his usual spot, killing the motor and headlights and sitting in silence for a long moment. Not knowing what he expected of her, Darcy sat motionless, suspense and anticipation building until she hardly dared to breathe.

"Sheila." He said the name slowly and shook his head. "Where are we headed this time?"

He sounded so forlorn, she reached for his hand to give comfort and was surprised when he jerked it away.

"I'm going for a swim," he said in a flat voice. "I'll see you in the morning."

"Swimming alone at night is dangerous." She was concerned about him; she wasn't fishing for an invitation to join him.

"Maybe, but not as dangerous as being with you."

He got out of the car and walked toward his cabin like a man carrying a heavy burden.

Darcy felt immeasurably sad, but also strangely glad. She didn't want him to be hurt again, and telling him the truth would surely do that.

CHAPTER FIVE

Noon in Michigan was nine A.M. in California. Sheila might still be in bed, but surely someone in the household would be awake. Darcy persuaded the business manager to let her use the box office phone during the lunch break, and now, as she waited for the credit card call to go through, she wondered at her sister's knack for getting accommodations from strangers. In Springfield, overnight invitations were reserved for relatives, old friends, and other special people. Darcy could never understand the casual hospitality Sheila enjoyed; it seemed like such an imposition to stay for days, even weeks, with someone she scarcely knew.

"Hoffman residence," a woman with a slightly English accent said.

"Could I speak to Sheila Simmons please?"

"Miss Simmons isn't available at the moment."

"This is her sister. If she's sleeping, could you possibly wake her for me? It really is important."

"Very well, I'll see." The woman didn't seem to relish the task.

Darcy tried not to clock the wait; she should've mentioned that the call was long distance.

"Hello," Sheila said at last, her voice still muffled with drowsiness.

"This is Darcy. When are you coming here?"

"Is that why you called me so early?"

Her sister's grumpiness about getting up to answer the

phone was too much for Darcy. "Do you have any idea what you've gotten me into? I need you here now!"

"I didn't know Nicky would be there. You can't blame me for that! You have no idea how crucial the situation is here." Sheila lowered her voice confidentially. "Tony said the decision could go either way. We have a big cocktail party tonight with some people I have to meet. I can't possibly leave when my whole career is hanging in the balance."

"That means you wouldn't have been there if I'd waited until evening to call!" Darcy had never felt so cross with her twin.

"Well, that depends on when you called. You still didn't have to get me out of bed."

"At least tell me what you know about Nick," Darcy urged.

"Oh, he's a brilliant director. He'll be doing *Sizzler* on Broadway next season. If he weren't so mad at me, I might be able to get a part in it. Is he still furious about our little breakup?"

"Yes," Darcy said woodenly. "How long were you with him? Why did you break up?"

"I was never exactly 'with him.' I mean, I didn't live with him. We were close, but he didn't understand that I couldn't see him exclusively if I wanted to get anywhere in the theater. He was terribly involved in a play with not even a tiny walk-on part for me."

Darcy hated what her sister was saying. Had Sheila changed so much since leaving home, or was Darcy really hearing her for the first time? Either way, her twin's opportunistic attitude bothered her.

"How is Nicky? You do have him fooled, don't you? Do be nice to him, Darcy, for my sake."

"He's fooled." Darcy despised herself too much to waste anger on her sister. "Tell me something about him."

"Of course, you should know how we met and all that. Well, he's thirty-three, no thirty-four. He studied theater arts somewhere in the East, Yale maybe. I get colleges mixed up. He's fantastically successful, always too busy to get married. His father does something dull, banking or something."

"Where did you meet him?" Darcy asked wearily, wondering if the dull pain she felt over one eye was going to become a full-blown headache.

"At a party on Long Island. I wore my violet velvet gown, the long one with the silver waist cincture—"

"Whose party?" Darcy interrupted impatiently.

"Oh, let's see. Someone Manny knows."

"Manny?"

"My agent, Manfred Zwarles. He took me there. The house belonged to Bloom-something. Bloomgard, Bloomgood, not Bloomingdale. Does it really matter?"

"No, I suppose not." Darcy rubbed her forehead, pressing one finger against the slight indentation at the corner of her eye in a futile attempt to ease the throbbing.

"I really like Nicky," Sheila said. "You won't make him any madder at me than he is, will you?"

"Sheila, how do you expect me to keep up this charade with a man who was your lover?"

"Lover? Darcy, you sound Victorian! We had some fun, that's all."

"It was more than that to him," Darcy muttered softly. Sheila didn't hear.

"You are doing the part all right, aren't you? There isn't a word to say. I don't see how you can do badly."

"There's quite a bit to it, even without lines."

"Well, I know you'll do a tremendous job, and I'll never be able to thank you enough. You're absolutely saving my life doing this!"

And ruining mine, Darcy thought, wishing she hadn't called her sister.

She didn't want lunch. Hoping fresh air would chase away her headache, she went to the lakeshore, took off her sandals and dug her toes into the sand, staring moodily across the small body of water. To the west heavy gray clouds were gathering, promising a storm before the day was over. The air was humid, without a whisper of wind.

The stifling air in the dining hall made her headache worse, and the heavy aroma of spicy spaghetti sauce simmering on the stove all afternoon was making her stomach feel queasy. She got through the rehearsal by letting her feelings for Nick show on her face whenever they were in a scene together. In spite of the threatening atmosphere as the storm moved closer, the cast was cheerful and optimistic about the play. With Brett gone, Cole was docile and cooperative, and Constance's enthusiasm was infectious. Darcy tried hard to throw herself into *Wings of Love*, and the effort exhausted her. When Nick finally called it quits for the day, she hurried to the solitude of her cabin.

Bathing her face in cool water, she peered in the small framed mirror over the sink, appalled by the dark circles under her eyes. Tension and atmospheric pressure had combined to give her the worst headache of her life, so severe it was almost blinding. Wetting a washcloth with cold water, she pressed it across her brow and lay on the bed, wishing she had something stronger for pain than the aspirin she'd just swallowed.

It was more than the headache and the distant rumble of thunder that kept her from dozing. Pretending to be Sheila was extracting too high a price, and she was turning all her anger inward, blaming herself for letting her sister persuade her. Because she loved her twin, Darcy grieved for her, wishing Sheila weren't so caught up in chasing after success that people's feelings no longer mattered to her. Angry and disillusioned as Darcy was, she still felt compassion for her sister; Sheila was her own worst enemy, expecting more than most people were willing to give.

Nicky! Sheila's use of the nickname was offhand and intimate, hurting Darcy more than she wanted to admit. She moved the cloth to cover her eyes, shutting out the drab little room where she was going to have to wait out a thunderstorm alone. She hated lightning, the violent bolts of electricity splitting the horizon and felling trees. Her childhood pet, Ginger, a little mixed-breed dust mop of a dog, had been terrified of storms, pacing and panting even before they started, taking refuge under the bathroom sink, in a corner of the basement, or inside the fireplace. But there was no place for Darcy to hide.

Hating the thunder more than the heat, she dragged herself to first one window then the other, lowering and locking them to muffle the threatening din. Refreshing the cloth with cold water, she propped up the pillows and sank back, covering the top part of her face with the compress.

The rain began, big splotches that grew into a steady drumbeat on the shingled roof. Lightning lit the room for a heart-stopping instant, followed by a thunderous boom that made Darcy tremble. A storm was bad enough experienced from the confines of a sturdy brick building; here in a flimsy cabin flanked by giant trees that could crush it, she felt threatened and exposed. Telling herself she was silly didn't stop her from being paralyzed by fear.

A heavy thud sounded against the outside of the door; she couldn't remember locking it, nor could she force herself to walk six steps to open it.

"Shelia!" Nick burst into the room, bringing with him fresh rain-washed air and a foil-covered tray beaded with drops of water.

She sat upright, still clutching the cloth to her head, moved by something more powerful than fear of the storm.

"You didn't eat lunch," he said, forcing the door shut against the thrust of the wind. "When you didn't show up for dinner, I worried that you might be sick."

He set the tray on a small table beside the bed, moving her alarm clock to make room. "Mrs. Corning fixed some broth and sandwiches, something light, she said."

His face was wet, hair plastered to his scalp with a dark

fringe dripping on his brow. His jeans were water stained, and his shoes made slippery splotches on the floor. Shaking out the red windbreaker that had left his navy and white tank top only slightly damp, he hung it on the doorknob and sat beside her on the edge of the bed.

"Are you all right?" he asked.

"Just a headache."

"Eating something might help." He uncovered the tray, revealing plastic-wrapped sandwiches and a jelly jar full of dark amber liquid. "It's beef broth, I guess."

He stood and caught a drop of water that ran down his forehead, then found a towel on the rack by the sink and returned to the bedside drying his face and hair.

"Try some," he invited. "You shouldn't starve a headache." He unscrewed the cap on the glass jar and poured the contents into a plastic mug on the tray. "Just sip a little."

She complied but was too drained to enjoy the aromatic beef-stock broth with tiny slivers of carrot and onion floating on top.

"It's stifling in here." Nick was patting his neck and arms with the towel and using his fingers to comb through his thick hair, made wild by the rain.

"Be careful," she cried out involuntarily when he raised one window as far as it would go, letting a rush of rain-cooled air into the room.

"Of what?" He turned in surprise.

"The lightning."

He gave her a searching glance and returned to the bedside. "It's not raining in on that side. I'll leave it open. You're not eating."

"My head . . ." she said weakly.

"I didn't think you looked well this afternoon. Let me see if I can help."

He sat on the edge of the bed and removed his shoes, then slid to the end, resting his back against the footboard.

"Sit between my legs and I'll massage your neck. Sometimes that helps."

"No, I'd rather not, Nick."

The cool air in the room was forming cold beads of perspiration on her forehead, but it was Nick's presence that made her jittery now.

"Don't be silly." He took her hand and guided her between his outstretched legs, but it was his will not his arm that was pulling her.

With her back toward him, she could feel warm fingers caressing the nape of her neck, soothing away the tension. Pulling out her hair clips, he laid them aside and divided her hair down the middle, letting the parted hair fall forward on her shoulders.

"Isn't this better?" he murmured, his face so close she could feel his breath, a warm tickle on the back of her neck.

She reached for the towel he'd abandoned on the edge of the bed, but he took it from her, gently patting her face and neck until the cold film of moisture was gone and she felt less miserable.

"Now lean back against my chest," he ordered, shifting to accommodate her hips between his thighs.

His fingers on her brow were hypnotically soothing, lulling her into a semi-conscious state of contentment until lightning seemed to explode inside the cabin with a burst of unearthly light. She cried out without realizing it and burrowed into the only available refuge: the circle of Nick's arms.

"That was close," he said lightly.

"It was here!" she cried.

"No, darling, no. That was an optical illusion. The lightning is outside, far away. There's nothing to worry about."

Holding her, the strength from his arms seeping into her core, he crooned words of comfort, hardly realizing it when his murmurs became kisses, soft, whispering brushes against her neck and ears that inevitably found their way to her lips,

88

which were parted and trembling now under a wave of feeling more devastating than the storm.

How could she feel anything but warm in his arms? she thought. Every kiss was a message of comfort, enveloping her in his protective aura. At first relief and thankfulness made her press against him with newfound happiness, then she let herself be swept along, taking first his lower lip and then his upper between hers, making him groan with pleasure until he filled her mouth with a thrust of his tongue.

For an instant Darcy's spirit hovered over the man and woman locked together in a searing embrace and cried out a warning, but it was lost in a rush of uncontainable emotions.

Thunder rumbled over the cabin and rain bombarded the roof like the artillery of an advancing army, but Darcy's fear turned to wild abandonment, driving her even deeper into the arms of the man she loved.

With eyes closed, she let his lovely kisses dissolve the painful tension in her brow. His lips were cool on her lids, and little dots of light danced in front of her eyes. Sinking into a whirlpool of desire, she reached for him, needing the solid strength of his shoulders under her hands. His neck was soft and smooth above the hard ridge of collar bone, and she stroked it, feeling a pulse throbbing against her fingertips.

Their mouths met, his covering hers and gently drawing in the sweetness, teasing her with the passion he seemed to be fighting to control.

"Sheila," he murmured, nuzzling the hollow of her throat while his hand made lazy circles on her tummy, edging downward until she shuddered with longing.

This was the moment she'd promised herself would never happen. Nick was standing, hastily tossing his clothes onto the chair, turning back to her as a distant bolt of lightning bathed his bare chest in blue light. She opened her mouth to confess she was an impostor, but the words wouldn't come. Instead she sank back, limp and unresisting as he stripped off her clothing, garment after garment, caressing her satiny skin with warm urgent kisses. At last, after slowly rolling her panties over her thighs, his finger became a magic wand, making her burn with blind, raging desire.

Stretching out beside her, he took her in his arms, stunning her with the sheer joy of touching. The scent of his heated skin made her giddy with longing, and she squirmed against him, desperately wanting his warmth to be part of her. With his legs entwined with hers, Nick pressed his lips to her breast, savoring the silky softness of her nipple. Rainwashed air fanned their naked bodies, and the storm gradually rumbled away, leaving behind a gentle rain. The pitterpatter of raindrops on the roof were scarcely heard over their murmurs of love and the pounding of their hearts. He took her with tender urgency, his face hovering over hers, his eyes gleaming so brightly with passion and tenderness that she couldn't stop her tears. She couldn't believe how much she loved him.

The room was nearly dark, but she saw him clearly, his shoulders and arms tensed as he swayed over her in the rhythm of love. His mouth left hot kisses on her neck and shoulders as he thrust more deeply into her and she heard herself moaning with a fierce pleasure she'd never known before. Tightening her grasp on his shoulder with one hand and rubbing the other up the back of his neck, she felt herself swept along like melting snow in a mountain stream, becoming one with the torrential flow of Nick's loving. Her emotions overflowed like a great river flooding its banks, and she wanted to hold him forever, not feeling the burden of his weight in the afterglow of rapture.

He stirred and slid to her side, holding her, nuzzling her throat as he panted deeply, tickling her with his breath. When he dozed, his head grew heavy on her shoulder and his arm fell over her lower abdomen like a steel bar, but she fell asleep in a euphoric daze, aware only of the swell of his

90

shoulder, the contour of his hip, and the silky hair on the leg nestled between hers.

Her headache was gone, leaving only a supersensitive tightness over one eye. The storm, too, was only a memory, but Nick was curled beside her, sleeping quietly in the darkness, his skin filling her nostrils with sweet awareness of him. She loved him, but heartache was creeping through her, slowly eroding her deep sense of well-being. He still thought she was Sheila.

Her first impulse was to wake him and blurt out the whole truth, to beg his forgiveness. Maybe he loved Sheila enough to forgive them both, but the thought of telling him terrified her. He'd be humiliated. What man wanted to make love to a stand-in, to pour out his heart to a replica of the woman he loved? Sheila had hurt him deeply when she left him; how terrible it would be for Nick to know she'd also made a fool of him by substituting her sister for herself.

As if sensing her wakeful fretting, he turned to her, mumbling sleepily all the words Darcy wanted to be hers.

"I love you, darling. I didn't realize how much until tonight, but I do."

"Don't love me too much, Nick," she whispered, hugging him, hiding her face against his chest.

"You've changed," he said with awe. "You're all the woman I've ever wanted."

"Love me now," she said impulsively, feverishly eager to store up all the good memories possible until she was exposed as a fraud.

"Is your headache gone?" He pushed damp hair away from her forehead and kissed that spot that had ached unmercifully only hours earlier.

"Totally. Thanks to you."

"I don't think the massage did it." He kissed her, slowly flicking his tongue over her lips.

"No, it wasn't the massage."

91

"You must be starving." His voice was tender with concern.

"Only for you." It was true; food seemed to be part of another life, unneeded as long as she could lie in Nick's arms.

"I should take a shower." He held her closer, not wanting to leave her any more than she wanted him to go.

"Stay here."

He did.

Dawn came early, the gift of summer, filling the room with a golden light. Darcy didn't want to get up, much preferring to laze in bed and remember every moment of her night with Nick, becoming excited again in spite of her satiated lethargy. He was lying on his stomach, spread-eagled, taking far more than his share of the none-too-generous double bed. One of his legs imprisoned hers, and his shoulder and face were on her pillow. The spread and covers were bunched against the footboard, and the chilly morning air made her snuggle closer to him to share his warmth.

She'd never before woke up in bed with a man, but the thought of doing so morning after morning made her envious of married women for the first time in her life. Imagine, being able to reach out anytime she liked and feel Nick's muscular body and tousled hair. She couldn't resist caressing his back, letting her fingers trail down to the little hollow at the end of his spine. Wanting his attention, she patted his bottom. He groaned sleepily and rolled onto his back, taking her in his arms.

"Ready for a swim?" he asked.

"Sounds nice." She was ready for anything except losing him when he discovered the truth.

"I'd better get my suit. Mrs. Corning's crew comes to work too early to let us swim in the raw." He stretched lazily and made no move to leave.

"Yes, do get your suit." She couldn't see the clock but hoped it was very, very early.

"Maybe it's too cold to go in the lake," he suggested, cuddling against her, warming her with his length.

"A warm shower might be nicer." She kissed his throat and ran her fingers over the bristles on his chin, shadowy stubs of his morning beard. "Much nicer."

"I can't get over how much you've changed," he mused, taking her thumb in his fist and studying the back of her hand. "What happened here?" He fingered a small scar on her index finger, so faint now that only sharp scrutiny could detect it.

"I wanted to build a dollhouse, but I needed a few more lessons with the saw."

"I never pictured you playing with dolls."

Sheila never did. Darcy squirmed, but not from physical discomfort. Lying with Nick satisfied a need, a hunger she hadn't been aware of having. Cuddling even closer, she drank in his nearness like a thirst-crazed desert wanderer, dreading the moment when the day's activities would separate them, terrified of the time when he learned her true identity and rejected her.

"I guess all little girls go through a doll phase," she said.

He chuckled softly. "Funny, I could never picture you as a little girl either. Not until now anyway. I don't remember this tiny mole either." He touched a dark spot on her shoulder.

"Mole sounds awful! Couldn't you call it a beauty mark?"

"There's nothing about you that isn't beautiful." He stretched and spilled her onto her back, looking down on her with frank approval. "I can't understand it." He shook his head.

She was afraid to ask what puzzled him so much, but he told her anyway.

"I was sure you were selfish, overly ambitious, and about

as compassionate as a barracuda. How could I be so wrong?"

"You weren't wrong," she whispered miserably, her defenses crumbling.

The charade had to end! She was dying inside, wanting him so desperately that she was sacrificing her own principles.

"No?"

He did the worst possible thing, destroying her moment of moral courage by kissing her so deeply and tenderly that she melted against him, presenting herself as a love offering he was quick to accept.

Later, when she thought about it, their lovemaking at dawn was the sweetest of all, so slow it was almost indolent and so engulfing that their separate beings merged. She was willing to do anything to please him, but he demanded little, only that she love his lovemaking.

Not once during the hectic day that followed did she stop wanting him. Playing the part of Beth was a joy because she loved her leading man and wasn't afraid to let it show when they rehearsed their scenes.

"Good work today," Constance said after rehearsal, embarrassing Darcy because she hadn't been acting most of the time.

By unspoken agreement, she and Nick became secretive, unwilling to be the subjects of gossip and speculation. Darcy thought it was because their relationship was too special to share with others. They didn't eat meals together, and only their eyes communicated during the day. She could wait; when Nick's long day ended, he'd come to her.

Unfortunately it was a day of emergencies. The storm had done some damage to the roof over the backstage area, and Nick had trouble finding a roofer who would fix it right away. The business manager, who should have handled some of the problems caused by the storm, was called away because his father was critically ill. By the time Nick found an apprentice who was free to take over ticket sales, a large group of ticketholders for opening night wanted to cancel and reschedule for a night when seats were nearly sold out. One of the overheads was malfunctioning, and the lighting director left for Lansing to find a replacement.

When Darcy went to her cabin for the evening, Nick was still working with the cast of the musical. The male lead was a tremendous singer but a weak actor, and he was feuding with Harve, the assistant director of the musical. Again Nick was called upon to be a peacemaker, and Darcy marveled at his tact and perceptiveness in working with people.

Sitting on her bed, wearing a lacy pink nightgown and reading a paperback, she waited for Nick until her eyes drooped with fatigue, finally dropping the book and slumping back to sleep with the light on and the door unlocked.

When she awoke in the morning, the light was out and the place beside her was empty. Had he come at all? She raced to the switch and found that the light had been turned off; it didn't burn out. Nick had come, found her asleep, and left. She was deeply disappointed. With only a precious few days left before the play opened, she hated to waste any opportunity to be with him.

Was she being as selfish as Nick thought her sister was? she wondered. He must have been exhausted after a crisis-filled day. The absentee owner of the playhouse relied on the business manager and director to keep things going, expecting too much from people who already had their days filled with responsibilities.

Hoping that he'd come for her, she put on her swimsuit and brushed her hair into a ponytail high on her head. After a soft warning knock, Nick opened the door.

"You really should lock your door." His smile told her how much he missed her, but his kiss said it even better.

"Good morning," she said softly.

"I'm not sure I want to swim now." He held her close, sliding his fingers under the narrow straps on her shoulders.

"I missed you last night."

"You were sleeping so soundly, I didn't have the heart to wake you." He brushed his lips across her forehead. "We have so much to talk about."

"First let's swim."

Before they could really talk, she had to tell him the truth. Until then, she was determined to hang on to his love for just a little while longer.

"Get your towel." He smiled with fond indulgence, happy with anything that gave them precious moments together.

They didn't race this morning. Instead they swam at a leisurely pace, never far from each other, touching hands and feet, exchanging wet kisses and hungry caresses. He walked into a murky patch near shore to pick a water lily, sticking the stem down the front of her suit, cupping her breasts in his hands and inhaling the fragrance of the bloom. Teasing him, she did a water ballet, showing off the sleekness of her body, diving under him, evading him, finally coming into his arms.

"We'll miss breakfast," she said, not caring.

"You've missed too many meals. I like your new slimness, but I don't want you skinny." He led the way to the sandy strip where they'd left their towels.

This morning they didn't have the beach to themselves. Several apprentices, drawn to the water's edge by the early morning warmth, asked them how the water was and ran into the lake, the women squealing in mock shock and their male companions showing off with headlong plunges and fancy strokes.

"I have something important to ask you," Nick said, handing her a towel and ignoring the young swimmers in the water.

Darcy shivered, wrapping the towel around her shoulders, not cold but apprehensive. Nothing Nick could ask would solve her dilemma: the truth would ruin everything, but living a lie made her worse than Sheila.

"I'm freezing now," she fibbed.

"How about a warm shower?"

"Everyone will see if you come to my cabin," she said.

"I guess that really doesn't matter." He took her hand in his, finding her fingers cold.

"Let's go on like we did yesterday, keeping it our secret for just awhile longer."

"If that's what you want. . . ."

"For now anyway," she insisted.

"About my question . . ."

She started running, pulling him along, pretending not to hear. He left her at her cabin door.

The *Wings of Love* cast hurried away from the theater for lunch, leaving Nick and Darcy alone, facing each other across the stage.

"I have a feeling you've been avoiding me," he said, crossing the canvas floor toward her.

"No, I've just had to keep my mind on the sign language this morning."

"I thought you had it down pat." He grabbed a folding metal chair and sat on it backward, resting his arms on the back.

"No, I have to concentrate to remember it." This was true, because his nearness was a continual distraction.

"I've picked up a few words." He pointed toward his chest with an index finger.

"Me." She read his sign.

Crossing two closed hands, fingers straight, he pressed them to his heart.

"Love," she said softly.

He pointed away from his body with his index finger.

"You." She knew what his message would be, but it was oddly touching, delivered that way. "It's not difficult to sign *I*. Take the sign for *I* from the manual alphabet, a hand with only the little finger up, and put it on your chest."

97

He made the sign with a smile that told her more than any language could. "How do you make the sign for *want?*"

"Like this." With both hands in the position for the number *five,* she bent her fingers and drew them toward her body, smiling as he copied her gesture.

"And *need?*" he asked.

She quickly put her hand in position for the letter *X* and hooked her index finger downward.

"I'm impressed," he said. "Now I know all the important words: *I love you, I need you,* and *I want you."* He signed all three, pausing a little awkwardly between the words.

"Once you learn the hand shapes for the manual alphabet and the numbers, the rest comes easily."

"Some have to be spelled letter by letter?" he asked.

"There's a sign for fingerspell." She put her right hand palm downward and wiggled her fingers from left to right. "But the gestures take care of most ordinary conversation."

"You amaze me." He signed with crossed hands on his chest again. "I like the love sign. You really did study deafness to play this part, didn't you? I can't get over it."

She shrugged her shoulders. What could she say?

"There's so much I want to know about you," he said, resting his chin on his arms folded on the chair back. "Tell me about Springfield."

"The city's very proud of its Lincoln heritage." She couldn't bring herself to belittle her hometown the way Sheila always did.

"And you enjoyed growing up there?"

"Yes, I suppose so. I liked school."

Sheila didn't, she remembered.

"Tell me about your sister."

"Darcy? Why do you want to know about her?" Sheila wouldn't be interested in talking about her.

"Were you close?"

"I suppose so." Not as close as she'd thought, Darcy realized, finding the topic painful.

"I'd like to meet her."

"I'm sure you will someday."

"I didn't get a chance to ask you my question. What do you—"

"Nick!" Ken Davidson hurried through the backstage door, waving a thick manila envelope. "You told me to bring your mail as soon as it came."

Nick flashed Darcy a look of regret and moved to take the envelope, quickly ripping open the flap.

"Good, at least *Sizzler* is moving ahead as promised. I've been waiting for this information."

He leafed through a stack of pages, giving Darcy a moment to escape. She was halfway to the lodge when he caught up with her.

"You're running away."

"No, I'm just too hungry to miss lunch."

"We'll talk tonight," he said, glancing through the papers again. "I'd better take a sandwich back to my office and read through these right away."

Mrs. Corning was in a Mexican mood, serving straw hats —corn chips topped with spicy ground beef sauce and tangy grated cheese. The mixed fruit salad, honeydew and watermelon balls with sliced grapes and bananas, was a blessing to cool the tongue after the hot entrée, but food had nothing to do with the warm flush on Darcy's cheeks or the nervous agitation her hands betrayed, clasping and unclasping as she worried about Nick's question. Maybe her stolen paradise was going to end even sooner than she'd feared.

She went through the rest of the day with zombielike detachment, earning a mild rebuke from Nick when she failed to react for the third time in a scene they were rehearsing.

"I have things on my mind, too, darling," he whispered

99

when they were alone for their scene, "but let's not blow the play."

"No, I want to do my best."

She did want to give Nick a parting gift so he'd never forget her: a wonderful performance.

CHAPTER SIX

"Once a teacher, always a teacher," Constance said cheerfully. "What can I tell you?"

"I'm just curious," Darcy said. "What advice did you give your college students who were learning to act?"

They were talking by the lake, strolling on the beach after dinner.

"First I told them to observe the world, notice how voices and bodies work together to convey ideas and feelings. The two go together: it's not coincidence that actors are often good athletes. The discipline is much the same, but, of course, you know that."

Darcy had never thought of acting quite that way, but her favorite performers skied, raced cars, played tennis, and loved the outdoors. Many professional athletes went from sports to movies or television.

"What else did you say to your classes?"

Darcy kicked at a pebble with the toe of her sandal, wondering if her contrived casualness fooled Constance's professional instincts.

"Love," the ex-teacher said. "First you have to find something to love in yourself, then you have to love the character you're playing. Even a villain approves of some part of himself."

"Your classes must've been interesting."

"I tried, but there's nothing as exciting as acting itself.

You have to love it to succeed in this business. Love the stage, the play, and especially the people."

"That's quite a formula for success!"

"Speaking of success," Constance said, arching her brows, the most expressive Darcy had ever seen, "your scenes with Nick are going very well."

"Thank you."

Did Constance suspect that real love was the motivation whenever she was onstage with him? Eager to change the subject, Darcy asked, "Do you like theatre-in-the-round?"

"I love the closeness of the audience. Love! There's that word again! But we exist for the audience, you know; their approval makes us come alive. A good audience makes the performers excel. You must know it's a kind of ecstasy when everything is working; you know it, and the people out there know it! See how carried away I get!"

Darcy laughed with her, but her small parts in high school plays certainly hadn't carried her to any heights of rapture. She'd often wondered why the approval of an audience meant so much to Sheila, but Constance seemed to see it as a communion, a special kind of sharing.

"In our scenes, what would you have me do differently?" Darcy asked.

Constance frowned. "I'm going to direct the last play of the season with Harve's help after Nick leaves, but I'm not sure I should answer that question. If there's anyone in the business who knows what he's doing, it's Nick."

"He never says much to me about the play."

"A director isn't an acting teacher. Think of him as your first audience, someone who reacts to what's happening. It's harder when he's also playing a part."

"Did you study deafness before you did your part with the touring company?"

"I certainly did! I visited a school for the deaf, talked to teachers and students, read all the books I could find. Many deaf people have some hearing, you know, enough to be upsetting to them. A church organ can frighten an otherwise-deaf child."

"Deafness can make a person feel unwanted," Darcy added from her own experience. "Sometimes they pretend to hear just to please."

"In Act One, I think eagerness to please should dominate the scene in the corridor. Beth longs for the approval of her teacher."

"One thing in the play bothers me," Darcy said thoughtfully. "With modern teaching techniques, even children born deaf can learn to speak. They can develop new neuromuscular patterns. I don't know why Beth has to be portrayed as totally mute."

"I agree," Constance said. "The playwright ignored modern techniques for teaching the deaf."

"Of course, the theme of the play is becoming a whole person in spite of emotional pressures and physical handicaps. That wouldn't change if Beth did speak."

"Artistic license." Constance smiled and tossed a pebble, watching the ripples spread in a wide circle on the still surface of the water.

Darcy helped hem costumes for the musical, pitching in because she wanted to be part of the company, not just a guest player. Hiding away in the wardrobe room, she didn't see Nick all evening. Whatever his question was, she was in no hurry to hear it. Being a part of his world for a short time was becoming very important to her.

The theater was still lit but she didn't see Nick until he called out to her.

"Sheila, wait, I'll be down in a minute!"

He was on the bridge, a scary catwalk used to work the lights high above the stage. Afraid of heights herself, she was frozen with anxiety, watching him move with surefooted grace on the flimsy perch. If he fell, her world would end! She wanted to beg him to come down immediately, but all that she could whisper was "Be careful!"

103

Sighing with relief when he was safely down, she waited for him by the exit.

"Hot up there," he said, his face damp and the front of his white T-shirt sticking to his chest. "Give me time to take a shower, and we'll go for a ride."

She showered, glad to be leaving the grounds of the playhouse, slipped into a white cotton dress with narrow shoulder straps and a flaring skirt, and fastened a belt that matched the violets bordering the hem. Rejecting practical sandals, she put bare feet into the only dressy shoes she'd brought, high spike heels with slender white straps. After brushing her jet-black hair over her shoulders, she applied makeup with special care. Just once she wanted Nick to see her looking as attractive as possible.

In white slacks, loafers, and a dark brown silk shirt, he was handsome enough to fill her with bittersweet longing. What more could she ask of life than to belong with Nick? A smile battled with the tears building behind her eyes and won; she greeted him at her cabin door with unrestrained warmth, loving it when he kissed her lightly near the corner of her mouth so her lip coloring wouldn't smear.

"I thought we'd go someplace quiet tonight," he said.

"It's already after ten."

"When I'm with you, I don't seem to need sleep."

They drove the distance to Traverse City making companiable small talk, enjoying the breeze from the open windows.

"What do you think acting is?" she asked impulsively, remembering her conversation with Constance.

"Getting away with being another person," he answered without hesitation. "If you can do that, you're an actor."

His answer made her uncomfortable.

"If you were teaching a class, what advice would you give would-be actors?" she quizzed him.

"To let go of inhibitions. Shyness, hesitancy, tension— they all ruin concentration. You have to let go all the way, body, mind, and spirit, to be totally absorbed in the part you're playing. I imagine that sounds pretty basic to you."

According to what he said, she wasn't playing the part of Sheila well at all. Her own inhibitions were with her all the time, except when Nick held her in his arms. Part of what Constance said had hit home: she loved her sister, so she was able to play the role of Sheila. What no one could tell her was how to cope with anger and disappointment. She was furious at her twin for getting her into a deceitful situation, and just as angry at herself for agreeing to come to the Duckeye Playhouse. Worse, she didn't know how to handle the disappointment of finally meeting someone she could love wholeheartedly, only to know she'd lose him when he knew the truth.

The lounge, part of a motel complex, was dimly lit, with a piano player entertaining on a raised platform. He wore a silvery gray tux and sang every other verse, creating a romantic mood with his music. They were seated at a small table against the far wall, looking at each other over a candle sheltered by a hurricane globe.

Nick sipped bourbon and water while Darcy drank a powerful rum drink, a house specialty, a fruity concoction much stronger than the white wine she usually ordered. She knew she was becoming intoxicated; the music and Nick's closeness were intensifying the effect of the liquor.

"I have a crazy idea," he said.

"Oh?"

"Let's see if they have a room here."

Across from her, his eyes were half shut, the deep blue of the pupils invisible under the thick fringe of his lashes. His lips were relaxed in a faint smile, as though he knew an amusing secret. He reached across the table and took her hand in his, laying it palm down on the polished black surface, spreading her fingers and caressing the skin between them.

"What do you think?" he urged.

105

"Stay here? Tonight?"

"Suddenly I don't want to drive all the way back to Mallard Lake. I'll check at the registration desk."

Part of her approved and was eager to be alone with him. She tried to ignore a little whisper of doubt, watching him leave with a boyish eagerness in his step.

He came back dangling a room key and looking like a kid who'd just won the giant panda on a carnival midway. He dropped some money on the table for the cocktail waitress and offered her his hand.

"This is crazy," she whispered. "We can't check into a motel. We don't have any luggage."

"We just did. Our room is down this corridor."

The hallways crisscrossed like a maze, the carpeting changing from a dull rust to brighter orange with a brown floral pattern. They seemed to walk forever, his arm locked around her shoulders. She'd never gone to a motel with a man; knowing Nick was leading to one new experience after another.

"They had a last minute cancellation, otherwise we'd never have gotten a room at this time of year," he said. "You see, fate is in the driver's seat with us."

In that case she felt like a backseat driver, Darcy thought. There was something tacky about being in a motel room with Nick, even though it was attractively furnished with two large double beds covered by quilted navy and aqua spreads. The floor covering was a deep greenish aqua and the walls were papered in white with narrow silvery strips. Before Nick locked the door he hung a DO NOT DISTURB sign on the outside doorknob.

Darcy used the bathroom, scrubbing her face free of makeup and refreshing herself with vigorous splashes of cold water. When she came back, Nick had undressed and was stretched out under a crisp white sheet, his hands behind his head. Everything about him appealed to her, even the silky dark hair under his arms. For the thousandth time she wondered how Sheila could hurt a man like him, how she could leave him.

"Take off your dress," he said. "Please."

She did, hanging it carefully on a metal hanger, smoothing her half-slip over her hips.

"Now come here." His pleasure in looking at her softened the tone of command in his voice.

She couldn't move. Part of her wanted to be in his arms more than she wanted to live, but she was absolutely rooted to the spot, frozen like an ice statue, incapable of moving toward him.

"Is something wrong?" He sat forward in concern, puzzled by the odd expression on her face.

She shook her head, but it looked more like trembling than denial. Her chest ached and she was dizzy, not sure she was going to remain conscious.

"Sheila!" He ran to her side, pulling her against him. "Tell me what's wrong!"

She couldn't. Because she sometimes worked with children who were very tense, she recognized the symptoms of an anxiety attack but couldn't begin to explain it to Nick.

"I'd like to go," she said desperately.

"Sit here a minute first."

He guided her to the edge of the bed, but she refused to sit, standing beside it with stiff, unbending knees.

"Please, let's go back now," she begged.

"Sheila, what's wrong?"

The real Sheila could hold her liquor and was never indecisive. "I'm not feeling well," Darcy said, explaining the only way she could. Even her unflappable sister could get sick.

"I can see that. Lie down, and if you don't feel better, I'll call a doctor."

"No! Please, no, Nick. Just take me back to my cabin and I'll be fine."

107

"I don't understand." He shook his head gravely. "What's wrong? Are you in pain? Dizzy?"

"No—yes. I don't know! Please, get dressed and take me home."

Home was in Springfield, but he didn't seem to notice her mistake.

"Sure, if that's what you want." He was nice enough not to mention that he'd just paid resort rates for the room.

It wasn't what she wanted, but she couldn't stay and lie in Nick's arms pretending to be Sheila. Reaching for her dress, she pulled it over her head, refusing Nick's help. By the time she zipped up the back by herself and located her purse, he was dressed and ready to leave.

He guided her to the closest exit, explaining that an outside walk might make her feel better.

All the way back to the playhouse, she tried to find the right words to confess, hating herself as a coward and a fraud. Nick didn't help, fretting about her welfare and adding to her guilt with his kindness. When they parked in his usual spot, she considered getting into her own car and driving back to Springfield that night. Weariness and giddiness made her decide against it, and out of her misery came a new determination: a relationship with Nick might be hopeless, but she had the ability and the will to play the part of Beth. Before she left him forever, she was going to make the role of the deaf girl searching for herself come alive!

Nick opened the cabin with her key and stepped inside, but she didn't want him to close the door.

"Not tonight?" he asked unhappily.

"Please, no." His disappointment made her ache inside.

"I understand. If you need anything, you know where my cabin is. If there's anything I can do?" he asked, obviously reluctant to leave.

She longed to hug and comfort him, but all she could do was say good night. "I need sleep is all. I'm exhausted."

"Well, good night, darling." He kissed her tenderly and left.

Hot little tears leaked from her eyes, and she felt nothing but contempt for herself. If self-love was a part of acting, she was destined to fail there too. No! She had too much to bring to the part of the deaf girl: training, compassion, understanding, things that Sheila would consider irrelevant. Maybe Nick couldn't be hers under false pretenses, but the role could: She was determined to pour her whole heart and soul into making Beth's struggle a vital, sympathetic one. But all her resolve couldn't stop her from crying herself to sleep.

Avoiding a man when he's your director and leading man in a play that's about to open is no easy task, but Darcy tried. She waited until he left the lodge to run over for a hasty breakfast, skipped lunch, and avoided being alone with him during rehearsals. As opening night approached, he was too busy to do much about it. In the evening she undressed in the dark and didn't answer his knock on her cabin door. Her own fear of encountering Nick made her realize that there was an element of fear in everything Beth did in the play. Cautiously she began to tap more of her own emotions, using them to put her whole self into the part.

Nick refused to be avoided any longer. He called her into his office after the next morning's rehearsal, making it an order from director to actor.

"Your part is coming along well," he said impersonally, closing the door behind them. "You're showing a maturity I wouldn't have believed possible a year ago."

A year ago he didn't know Darcy Simmons, she thought.

Being in the same room with him was an ordeal. He was wearing faded blue shorts and a short-sleeve white shirt open down the front, slouching against the edge of the desk and jamming his hands into side pockets.

"But you're still as childish as ever if you think you can avoid me until this play closes," he said crossly.

"Why would I want to avoid you?" she asked, immediately realizing it was a foolish question.

"You tell me."

"I can't—there's no reason. I mean, I'm not avoiding you."

"Like hell you're not!" He straightened and grabbed her, kissing her furiously. "I could take it, if you'd put me off since you got here. Why pretend you care, then turn off your feelings like a faucet?"

"That's not what I'm doing!"

"No, then tell me how you feel about this!" He took her in his arms, ignoring her stiffness.

She felt breathless and tormented, loving him so much that his angry kisses seared her conscience, erasing in moments all the barriers she'd been erecting between them.

"There," he said, holding her so close she could feel the breath expanding his lungs. "There," he repeated.

"People say 'there' after they finish a job!" She wiped a hand across her mouth, wanting to preserve, not eradicate, the minty taste of his kiss.

"That was a satisfied 'there.' You're not as indifferent as you've been pretending to be."

Indifferent! She could never be that, but he was making her angry, testing her reaction as if all that mattered was the state of her hormones!

"Just because you spent one night in my cabin doesn't mean I want you there all the time."

"Spent the night! We made love, Sheila. Love, that's the operative word. You weren't faking. You weren't acting or pretending. I know it meant as much to you as it did to me." His face was ruddy with anger, his lips drawn tight, and his eyes narrowed in disbelief. "You wanted me as much as I wanted you. And I've never said a corny line like that before!"

Remembering his earnest efforts at sign language, she was afraid she'd begin to cry. *Want* was such a gritty word, full of undercurrents and pitfalls. Of course she wanted him, but as soon as he knew her identity, he'd hate her. She wouldn't be strong enough to stay and finish the play. Precious days near him would be lost, and all the emotional turmoil she was pouring into the part of Beth would go to waste. Stubbornly she stood her ground, letting silence be her response.

"I never asked you my question," he said, settling one hip against the desk, attempting to appear relaxed but not succeeding.

"No, you didn't." She dreaded hearing it.

"First let me ask, what do you plan to do when *Wings of Love* closes?"

"I'm not sure. There's a possibility—that is, I may have a movie part."

"You're chasing movie roles again." His voice was heavy with scorn.

"There's nothing wrong with films!"

"Nothing at all! Take off enough clothes and you'll be a big hit—until your rear starts to sag and you need a bra to look young. Damn it, Sheila, you never listen to anything you don't want to hear! Learn your craft first! In Hollywood you'll just be a new pair of tits!"

Her hand resounded against his cheek, stunning her more than it surprised him. To her horror, she'd reacted exactly as Sheila would, attacking him for his truthfulness.

"I'm sorry," she stammered miserably.

He rubbed his cheek and studied her, the vivid blue of his eyes icy with anger. "You're sorry because you're not sure I won't hit back."

"No." She shook her head, remorseful but not afraid of what he'd do.

"I warned you once before not to slap me," he said with quiet menace.

He took her wrist in an unbreakable grasp, making her realize how little she knew about the man she loved.

111

"I didn't mean to," she said without much hope of being believed.

"I probably asked for it this time," he said gruffly, taking her in his arms, "but don't ever hit me again, Sheila. I swear, I'll spank you."

His threat conjured up an uncomfortable image, and she could visualize dangling over his knees while he swatted her bottom. That was something Sheila deserved, not her! Then his lips were on hers, moving gently over them while he stretched the elastic of her red nylon shorts, slipping under the band of her panties, kneading the firm globes of flesh with his strong fingers. Crushed against him, she ignored the warning sounding in her head, thrilled by his audacity, even though her saner self knew that now he did deserve a slap.

Her slippery shorts were sliding downward, caught above her knees, and she suddenly felt silly. Did he expect her to lie on his desk in broad daylight with her panties around her ankles? Her dignity would suffer as much as if he had spanked her, and she wasn't at all sure making love on the hard old oak desktop wouldn't have the same effect.

"No, Nick, please, no." Her words came out hesitantly.

"Yes, Sheila, thank you, yes."

He was punishing her, getting even for the slap as surely as if he'd slapped back! She was so furious she nearly forgot herself and walloped him again, instead struggling away from his arms and trying to inch up her shorts at the same time. Her life had hit a new low; she was being mauled by a man who thought she was Sheila, and her insides were jumping around like corn in a popper. Nick bedeviled her as she tried to get her clothing back in order, but his intimacies were outrageous, not loving.

"I'm hungry, I'm going to lunch," she said loudly, flushing under his instant burst of laughter.

"I'll get some sandwiches, and we can go to my cabin."

"No, no way!"

"You'll regret it, darling. We have a long day's work

112

ahead of us before we can be alone again. Won't you be thinking about what you're missing?"

"No! I regret a lot of things," she said trying to tuck her shirt back in place. "Leaving now won't be one of them."

"You haven't heard my question yet, my reason for inviting you to my office."

"Invited! You ordered me!"

"Will you stay now if I order you to?"

"Absolutely not!"

"Then you must have accepted my invitation of your own free will."

"I don't want to play word games with you, Nick."

"You don't play any game you know you'll lose." He was blocking the door without trying to touch her again.

"Let me go."

"My question first."

"The answer is no!"

"You haven't heard the question yet."

"I don't want to hear it." She wanted to run, or better yet, scream, to drive away the memory of his assault on her senses.

"Then I don't think I'll ask."

"Ask, so I can say no and be done with it."

"No, you're in a hurry. Forget it!"

"Ask me, Nick! Stop teasing!"

"You're not in the mood for this question."

"I never will be, so tell me what it is!"

He shook his head.

"Then don't." Her hand was on the metal doorknob.

"Later this evening," he said.

"No."

"Now or never?"

"This is ridiculous!" She slammed the door behind her, hearing the echo of his laugh all the way to the lodge where nearly everyone was finishing a lunch of hot dogs, split to hold cheese and wrapped in bacon. Nick came a few minutes later but didn't sit at her table.

"A good dress rehearsal is one where everything possible goes wrong," Constance said, relaxing for a minute between acts in the dressing room.

"Then this one must be terrific," Darcy said without thinking, remembering too late that rehearsals were old stuff to Sheila.

"Cole will get his voice back by tomorrow night. He's enjoying the sympathy and attention tonight, but he'll make a fast recovery, you watch."

"What if he doesn't?" Darcy asked with concern.

"I imagine someone else will fill in."

"As my father? Most of the men here are younger than me!"

"Harve has a deep voice. He could manage."

Darcy knew why she was so worried about Cole's sore throat: the play was vitally important to her now. Its success meant everything.

The technical rehearsal the night before had dragged, mainly because perfecting the lighting, staging, sound, timing, and use of properties was the objective. The players went through their parts with a noticeable lack of spirit after a temperamental light switch caused annoying delays. Hopefully, Darcy thought, the second act would go well in their last practice run, superstitions about bad dress rehearsals notwithstanding.

Nick was avoiding her now. Since their confrontation in his office, he only spoke to her during rehearsals. Neither hostile nor cordial, he didn't seem to be aware of her at all. She was conscious of wasted minutes and squandered hours when they could have been together. The play would open Friday, run for a week, and close the following weekend with an early curtain on Sunday evening that would be well-

114

attended by senior citizens bused in by special arrangement. After that Darcy would leave.

Before Nick had asked about her plans, she'd pushed aside thoughts of the remainder of the summer. A group from the Springfield area was going on a hiking trip in the Rockies. Her deposit was paid, and before meeting Nick she'd been excited about joining the twenty young men and women for two weeks of outdoor living. One of the men lived in Moline, and they'd had coffee after an organizational meeting. He'd phoned her several times and they were both looking forward to becoming better acquainted on the trip. Her life wasn't as glamorous as Sheila's, she mused, but it satisfied her. She loved her job, enjoyed her friends, and didn't need Nicholas Cross.

Making the sign for need, she watched her reflection in the dressing room mirror, a technique helpful to people learning sign language but depressing to Darcy. Her hair was parted in the middle and coiled over both ears, a severe style that she wasn't sure was right for Beth. With her eyes heavily shadowed and her fair skin darkened by makeup, she reminded herself of a heroine in a nineteenth-century melodrama. She didn't want to debate with Hilda, the stylist who did her hair, but she was sure Beth would wear a looser, more modern hairstyle. Maybe Nick would let her uncoil it for the last scene as a symbol of Beth's new quest for fulfillment, she thought. The gray skirt she was wearing was too long, and the gray-and-pink flowered blouse was too matronly for the character. Beth was physically handicapped and emotionally harassed, but that didn't mean she had to dress like someone's grandmother.

"Do you like this costume?" Darcy asked Constance.

Her friend frowned. "It's a trifle long."

"In your touring company, what did Beth wear in Act Two, Scene One?"

Constance arched her brows, showing her reluctance to

115

give an answer that made the Duckeye production seem less professional. "Nick knows what he's doing, Darcy."

"Yes, but what did she wear?"

"A yellow dress, if I remember correctly. A very plain dress."

"But not frumpy, I'll bet," Darcy insisted.

Nick was talking with the stage manager, Ken Davidson, whose unenviable job it was to see that the whole production came off without a hitch. At this point, much of the show's success depended on his alertness and attention to detail. Darcy was nervous about her role but wouldn't want to change places with the person who had to keep track of everything.

She waited until the two men finished talking, both too absorbed in their responsibilities to acknowledge her, then touched Nick's arm when Ken walked away.

"Curtain in three minutes," he said impatiently. "I have to change my shirt."

He was hurrying toward the men's dressing room with Darcy at his heels.

"What is it?" he asked, casting off one shirt as he ducked through the curtain and coming out again immediately, putting on David's Act I top.

She followed him again as he hurried toward the entrance to the stage ramp.

"This costume, Nick. Don't you think it's too old for Beth?"

"No."

"She's repressed and confused, but she doesn't have to dress like a drudge. And no one wears her hair this way anymore."

"Sheila, this is a poor time to suggest a costume change."

"Can we talk about it after the rehearsal?"

"Places," Ken ordered.

"Yes, yes, but you know better than to make changes at this point."

116

"I didn't realize how awful I look."

"There won't be any Hollywood scouts here," he snapped. "Try concentrating on your part and forget about showing off how pretty you are."

"That's not why I want a change!"

Ken shushed her with an impatient gesture.

"I don't think Beth would fix her hair like this or wear such an awful outfit. She's deaf, not blind," she whispered hurriedly. Nick's angry silence made her even more determined to change her costume.

She gave the second act all she had, concentrating with every ounce of determination, becoming Beth as the emotional net tightened around her. In the last scene real tears ran down her cheeks because she keenly felt what was happening to her character.

Hurrying off afterward, she was totally drained, not believing she could give the same performance night after night through a full week and an extra weekend. Finishing the second act had been like running in front of a steamroller on hot asphalt; her clothes were soaked.

"Sheila." Nick came up to her, a softer expression on his face. "You were tremendous in the last scene."

She had enough sense to quietly thank him instead of voicing her doubts about the coming performances.

"Now, what about your costume?" he asked.

"It's this one," she said pulling the damp, rumpled blouse loose from her throat. "Don't you think it's too matronly for Beth? She's sheltered, but that doesn't mean she has to look so dumpy."

"I hate to pull a wardrobe switch at this point, but you could be right. Walk over there and let me see." He pointed at a pile of furniture odds and ends stacked against a workroom wall. "Now turn around slowly."

Was he studying the costume or the swing of her hips as she slowly obeyed him? She felt terribly self-conscious under his gaze, wondering if his decision was really taking so long.

"All right," he said. "It is a little drab. Did you have something else in mind?"

"I saw a pink flared skirt in the storage room. If it fits, I can wear my own white knit top with it."

"Nothing sexy or revealing," he warned.

She gave him an angry scowl but didn't want to argue after he'd conceded to her.

"Let me see the skirt."

"It's just a plain—"

"I want to see it."

She braved the wardrobe head's jaundiced stare; there were no secrets backstage, and the woman already knew that a visiting actress wanted a last minute change. Darcy felt intimidated but refused to let it show.

The pink skirt was a little too long for Darcy's taste, but Nick said it would do if she really wanted to switch.

"I'm coming over to your cabin when I'm done here," he said, sounding just as authoritarian as he had about the skirt.

"Do I have a choice?"

"About letting me in? I suppose you do, but we're both going to look silly shouting at each other through those little windows."

"All right, but only for a few minutes. I'm beat."

"Do you think you're the only one who's tired?"

Dress rehearsal certainly brought out the bear in him, she thought, and flounced away, his attitude robbing her of a sense of victory over the costume change. At least she had the satisfaction of knowing that she'd been convincing as Beth.

Showering slowly, pampering her weary body with as many suds as the hard water allowed, she let the warm spray beat full force on her tight muscles. Turning off the hot water first to avoid being scalded, she didn't move fast enough to duck the full force of the cold in the tiny stall. Shivering, she hurriedly scampered out and swished the towel over her body. Sitting on the edge of the bed, she dried her limbs, patting her feet and poking a corner of the towel between each toe, wishing she could go home and soak in her own tub. Then, using a big fragrant mitt, she powdered herself from neck to feet, feeling pampered and silky-skinned. Nick knocked on the door while she was still naked.

"Just a minute," she called. She didn't have a robe with her, so she slipped into a cotton nightie, white with orange dots and long enough to cover her knees.

"It smells nice in here. Is it you?" He stepped into the room, banging the door shut behind him. "You have powder on your cheek."

He reached out and brushed it away.

"What do you want, Nick?"

He looked hot, his face gleaming and his hair moist and tousled; the summer was promising to be unusually warm in northern Michigan. Shaking his head, he sat on the edge of the bed.

"I still haven't asked you my question."

"Are you sure this is the right time?" She didn't want anything to stop her from opening in the play the next evening.

"No, but there may not be a right time." He reached for her hand and studied her wrist, which was covered with the fine, fragrant white powder. "You have powder everywhere."

"Just about. It makes me feel cool and dry."

"I'd like to feel that way. I haven't felt cool since you came here."

"I'll loan you my powder mitt."

"I wouldn't know what to do with it," he said with mock innocence. "Of course, if your services come with it . . ."

"If you think I'll powder you like some overgrown baby—"

"The thought crossed my mind," he admitted.

Was he ever going to ask his dreadful question? she wondered. But when he stood and took her in his arms, she stopped caring about anything but the heat of his body and the pressure of his lips on hers.

"You're too clean to kiss," he whispered, covering her breasts with his hands, playing with the cloth of her nightie.

"I'm hot again," she murmured.

"I'd like to know if you have any plans for the rest of the summer," he said gravely, resting his arms on her shoulders, making a yoke to bind her to him.

"I'm not sure." She moistened her lower lip with the tip of her tongue.

"I have a suggestion."

She was afraid to hear it.

"We really do have something going for us this time, don't we?" His eyes were so searching, she didn't dare meet his gaze.

"Yes." It was the truest word she'd ever spoken.

"I don't know where we're headed, but I'd like time to find out. Will you stay here the rest of the summer until I leave, Sheila?"

His words laid a burden on her heart, and she didn't know how to answer.

"You want to, don't you?" he asked softly.

"Yes. But I don't think I can. Nick, things aren't quite what they seem—"

"Don't say no now!" He brushed his nose against hers, nipping at her lips with little love bites.

"I have to tell you—"

"No, just think about staying. That's all I ask. There aren't any big parts available, but I'm sure I can fit you in somewhere. But I don't want you here as a performer, only as the woman I love."

"Oh, Nick, please let me tell you—"

"No." His kiss sealed her lips, then his lips ranged freely over her face until she melted with longing.

"There are probably a hundred good arguments why you should get on with your life as soon as the play closes, and there's only one reason for staying: I want you to."

It was the most persuasive argument she'd ever heard, but the offer wasn't hers to accept. It belonged to her sister.

"Nick, please listen—"

"No, I'm leaving now so you can't give me any excuses. Just think about a whole summer together. My cabin is bigger than this one and my bed is better; say yes and I'll help you move."

He kissed her again, slowly and deeply, burying his hands in the long strands of hair already beginning to dry.

"I know a summer at the Duckeye won't make you a famous star, darling, but I promise you'll wake up smiling each and every morning," he whispered against her cheek.

His good-night kiss made her toes curl, but he had every intention of leaving her cabin. He was strong enough for both of them, even though she rubbed against him like a kitten looking for a home.

"Good night," he whispered, unable to resist one more quiet kiss. "Think about what a whole summer could mean to us. Think hard."

Darcy did little else all night, even though she knew she needed sleep to perform well. Nick was with her through the long late hours as surely as if he slept beside her.

At last she'd been ready to tell him, praying that some small measure of his affection would survive when he knew the truth, but he'd refused to listen.

CHAPTER SEVEN

The best thing about opening night was that no rehearsals were scheduled during the day. The cast members were free to relax, and to most of them this meant sleeping late. Darcy slept long beyond her usual time, glad she'd at least gotten some rest after hours of restless tossing and fretting.

Walking to the lodge, hoping for a cup of coffee even though it was past time for breakfast, she heard a shrill screech from the beach. It was also a holiday for the three apprentices in *Wings of Love,* and Raleigh was continuing his good-natured pursuit of Sue as they played in the water. Darcy wondered if Nick had taken an early morning swim.

Cole was sitting with Constance, his throat wrapped in an ivory silk scarf. He seemed to be communicating mainly with gestures, so Darcy hurried to their table after picking up a bun and a cup of coffee put aside for the late risers.

"Will your voice be all right?" she asked anxiously.

Cole nodded and let Constance speak for him.

"He'll be able to perform, if he rests his voice until to-night."

"That's good news," Darcy said.

She bit into a sticky pecan bun, not her usual morning fare but she was ravenous. Acute nervousness gave her an appetite, and she'd never been quite so anxious about anything as she was about *Wings of Love.* She wasn't stagestruck, and it didn't matter if she never did another play. It was the part of

Beth that was so important to her; she wanted to make the character come alive.

"You were right," she said to Constance.

"I was? About what?"

"Loving your character. I love Beth. She's become terribly special to me."

"It shows. I can't believe how much you've developed your part since the first rehearsal."

"I was pretty awful that day!"

Cole made a hissing sound of agreement, vigorously nodding his head, unwilling to be left out of any discussion for very long, voice or no voice.

"It's not where you begin; it's where you finish that counts," Constance said philosophically, tempering her serious tone with a brief grin.

The phone was ringing in the kitchen, deserted now while Mrs. Corning and her crew took a mid-morning break.

"I'll get it," Constance said. "I'm expecting a call from my agent."

Darcy finished her bun and drank her coffee, not up to carrying on a one-sided conversation with Cole. When he found her attention straying, he carefully rearranged the folds of silk around his throat and left. How his neck could get chilled on a day that promised temperatures in the high, humid eighties, she didn't know.

"Darcy, the phone is for you," Constance called, motioning her toward the kitchen, then leaving.

Only her parents and Sheila knew where she was. She picked up the receiver with misgivings.

"Hello."

"Darcy, it's Sheila. I'll be able to do the part after all, at least in most of the performances. It opens tonight, right?"

"Oh, no!" Darcy gasped.

She was devastated. Beth was her part! Sheila couldn't grab it away after everything she'd been through.

"I'm disgusted with Hollywood," her sister said, ignoring

Darcy's stricken protest. "People here are not to be believed."

"You didn't get the part?"

"I never said it was a sure thing. Tony's friends have been a big disappointment, and so has he. I'm on standby for a flight to Chicago. From there I'll have to make connections."

"Sheila, don't come. Let me finish the play. I think I'm good in it."

"Well, of course you are, but you're not a professional. People think you're me! Imagine how that makes me feel. The audience will judge me on how well you do."

"That didn't bother you when you begged me to come here."

"It did bother me. I just couldn't be in two places at the same time. Darcy, how are you getting along with Nick?" Her sister sounded anxious.

"Fine. No problem." This was one lie that didn't make Darcy feel guilty.

"He's opening a new play on Broadway. Oh, I know there won't be anything big in it for me, but I'm willing to take anything at this point. So you see how important it is that I get there as soon as possible."

"He'll wonder why you've changed the part so much from the way I've rehearsed it."

"Oh, I'll handle that. I'll tell him I haven't been feeling well, but now I'm better and ready to do the part the way it should be done."

"Sheila, listen, please." Nick was right—her sister only heard what she wanted to hear. "I'm doing the part well. I'm sure of it. You have to let me finish. It won't hurt your career, and you owe me that much."

"I don't care about the part, but I need to see Nick again."

"See him later in New York."

"That will be too late. What has he said about me? About him and me?"

"He was furious when you left him."

"I suppose he was, but he couldn't expect me to give up my career, could he? Darcy, I have to get ready to leave. I'm not sure when I'll get there, so I'll rent a car and come right to the playhouse."

"And have everyone see two Sheila Simmonses?"

"No, of course not. I have my blond wig with me. If there's a seat left for tonight's performance, have the box office save it for me under the name of—let's see—Diana Harris. It will help me a lot if I can see *Wings* once before I take over the part. Where are you sleeping?"

"Sheila, you're not being fair!"

"I told you I'd come as soon as possible. That was part of our agreement."

"The only thing I agreed to do was come here and be in the play."

"Until I could take over! I'm calling from a pay phone, Darcy. We'll have to talk about all this when I get there. And try to remember everything Nick has said to you. I want to know all about him. Is he still mad, do you think?"

"Sheila, don't come here—"

The line went dead in her ear, and she felt like shrieking in frustration. Sheila owed her a chance to stay in the play. She had no right to come back to Nick, not now. Darcy clenched her fists on the counter, too upset to think straight.

Standing outside the lodge, she felt like a marionette without strings, helpless to ward off impending disaster. If she told Nick the truth now, she thought, it would seem like taking revenge against Sheila. But Darcy had more to lose than her sister: Nick's respect. Telling him would put him in the middle of a sisterly quarrel. Somehow she had to handle Sheila another way. One thing was sure: her sister was on the way and Darcy couldn't stop her.

Should she reserve a ticket for her? A few seats were still

available. Maybe if Sheila saw how well she was doing in the part, she would decide against taking it away from her. It was a feeble hope.

Glum and downhearted, Darcy walked around the theater to the outside window of the box office, asking the person manning it for a one-seat reservation. What name had Sheila suggested? Diana—yes, Diana Harris. The ticket was for a back-row seat, Darcy noticed. She didn't pay for it. If Sheila didn't claim it half an hour before the performance, it could be sold to someone else.

The grounds of the playhouse were too confining, and she didn't want to talk to anyone, not when there was a possibility that everyone would soon learn what a fraud she was. Wearing her bathing suit under a denim skirt and loose cotton blouse, she drove west toward Lake Michigan, welcoming the time alone and feeling fortunate when she located a public beach that wasn't overly crowded.

Stripping down to her suit in the car, she carried only a towel and purse across the hot sandy beach. A couple of young mothers were watching their children build castles in the wet sand near the water's edge, and Darcy was afraid she'd been doing much the same thing with Nick—creating fantasies that would wash away as easily as the tide would destroy the children's castles.

Walking until she found a spot with no one near, she spread her towel and sat staring at the far horizon where the clear blue of the sky blended with the beguiling blue-green color of the lake. In the distance the long silhouette of a lake freighter was moving south, down to the steel mills of Gary, its elongated hull a sliver on the horizon.

Solitude was no answer to her dilemma. She waded in the icy swells near shore but didn't swim. The season was still too young for the water of the Great Lakes to be warm. Not trusting the undertow in this unfamiliar body of water, she stayed close to the beach.

An hour in the sun was more than enough; she didn't

126

want to add sunburn to her other problems. Quickly becoming weary of her own company, she headed back toward the playhouse, wishing there were a solution awaiting her at the end of her drive. Substituting for Sheila had been a bad mistake; falling in love with Nick was an even worse detour from the orderly course of her life. What happened next could change everything, but she was thinking with her heart, not her head. Love for Nick and pride in the way she was portraying Beth were somehow intertwined, and she needed to see the play through to the end of its run in order to let her emotions crystallize.

Parking the car, she went to her cabin, intending to shower and rinse the sand out of her suit.

Was she the one who was being selfish now? Acting was Sheila's career; Darcy's only reason for coming to the Duckeye had been to help her sister. Naturally Sheila expected her to step aside now that the opportunity in California had fallen through.

Dressed in clean white shorts and a navy top, Darcy carried her wet suit outside to hang it on a clothesline behind the lodge, where the sun could dry it. The cast of *Carousel* was working harder than ever, and the players in *Wings of Love* were enjoying their free day somewhere out of sight. Behind the lodge the woods were cool and inviting, the bed of the forest dotted with lacy ferns. At the far right a narrow path was covered with last season's dried and matted leaves, nature's natural carpeting.

Darcy could understand why fables so often spoke of enchanted forests. This woodland beckoned, inviting her to enter the shadowy bower. Wearing sandals and shorts, she wasn't dressed for tramping the woods, but she decided there couldn't be any harm in wandering down the path a short way. Even if it curved and branched, she was an observant hiker who rarely lost her sense of direction.

The path wasn't quite as clear as it seemed, and she had to walk carefully to avoid roots swelling out of the ground and small branches waiting to hook onto the straps of her sandals. Little nosegays of wildflowers nestled under the trees, tiny purple and white blooms that no devoted naturalist like Darcy would dream of picking. The narrow trail did branch, with the left turn meandering along a ravine. Darcy stared down at a trickle of a stream in a great gully of raw earth strewn with water-smoothed boulders. The descent was too steep to attempt wearing sandals, but being alone in the cool, dim woods was balm for her spirit.

There was no reason to hurry back; she had nothing to do until dinner. The path skirted the ravine, then angled sharply downward, narrowing to a lightly trampled trail. Darcy liked to imagine a lone Indian brave in deerskin moccasins running silently over an invisible path deep in the forest, living off the bounty of the land and communing with woodland spirits.

Perhaps she was wandering too far, she thought. The trail was almost nonexistent now, and she had to concentrate to retrace her steps to the ravine, somehow becoming confused and ending up on the wrong side. She couldn't cross this natural barrier, so she had to backtrack to discover the original path. The nap she'd hoped to take before dinner would have to be forgotten. If she didn't hurry, she wouldn't even have time to eat.

She reached the original fork just as a noise shattered the peaceful hush. Straining to hear, she hoped this wasn't bear country. When she recognized her own name reverberating through the trees, she changed her mind; a grizzly wasn't as awesome as the man calling her.

"Over here," she called out, standing still and waiting for him.

Nick didn't exactly crash through the woods, but he managed to stir leaves and snap branches.

"Thank God!" he said. "When you decide to disappear, you really make a production of it!"

"I thought this was a free day."

"Free from rehearsals." He stepped close and put one hand on her shoulder. "That doesn't mean you have to drive me crazy by vanishing. First your car was gone, then it was back. I've done everything but drag the lake looking for you."

"How did you know I was here?"

"My Boy Scout training. I saw your bathing suit on the line, and this is the closest path into the woods. What're you doing here?"

"Just walking. Why did you want me?"

"You've already missed dinner. We have something called a play to perform tonight."

"What time is it?"

Her watch said five twenty-six.

"Not quite five thirty, but dinner is early on show nights. I told you yesterday."

"I completely forgot! Nick, I'm sorry. I was on my way back now."

"No harm done. Mrs. Corning is keeping a plate hot for you, and we're in the perfect place to do this."

He swept her into his arms, kissing her soundly and crushing her against him.

"That's for luck," he said softly, brushing aside thick waves of hair to nuzzle her ear. "And this is for me."

His repertoire of kisses never failed to surprise her; this kiss sank into her mouth and aroused every inch of her body. Responding eagerly, she drew his lips between hers, not holding back, letting all her tension and stress drain away as she felt herself become a part of him again.

"Darling." He hugged her even closer. "I wish we had more time."

"We do have to hurry, don't we?" She made him back off first, not able to bear even a momentary parting.

"There's something else we have to do as soon as the show is over."

"What?"

129

"Talk about the rest of the summer. I couldn't sleep last night, worrying about whether you'll decide to stay here with me."

"I don't—"

"No, not now. I'm not going to take no for an answer, so let's leave it until after the curtain."

The path was too narrow to walk side by side, but he was close behind her, caressing her shoulder, catching her hand for a gentle squeeze, warning her about branches and obstacles with chivalrous concern. She wished she could tell him about rafting on the Colorado and winter camping in the mountains, but Sheila never want any place that didn't have a Holiday Inn. After the play they would talk, but she didn't share his anticipation.

Oh, my darling, she silently cried, how can I hurt you with the truth? She wished there was some way to spare him the agony of knowing he'd been deceived.

"Oh, I forgot," he said, stepping beside her at the edge of the clearing. "You had a phone call earlier this afternoon. She left a message."

"Did you take the call?"

"No, Mrs. Corning did. She told me when she didn't see you at dinner. Diana someone . . ."

"Harris?"

"Yes, I think so. She was calling from Chicago. That was the message: she was calling from Chicago."

Her last hope died; Sheila wasn't stuck on the coast, still trying to get a flight. With her luck, Darcy thought, she'd probably step off one plane and onto another for shuttle service to Traverse City. She was going to be at the Duckeye for opening night.

"Thank you," she said to Nick in a guarded voice.

He shrugged, more interested in the refreshing beauty of the woman beside him than in the phone message.

Stage fright is an insidious monster, Darcy learned. One moment she was behaving like a normal person under mild

130

stress, and the next she was filled with horrendous fears, sure that the entrance ramp would collapse when she stepped on it and the stage would heave up like a great white whale and topple her into an eternal purgatory reserved for terrified actors.

Her face was perspiring so profusely she had to hold a cold cloth over it, until her skin cooled enough to put on makeup without having it melt. After the correct makeup had been demonstrated for them at the dress rehearsal, the actors were supposed to do most of it themselves; everyone else in the cast was an experienced professional who found this relatively easy to do. The apprentices, Sue and Jeanette, were doing each other because Jeanette was too farsighted to do a good job on herself. Knowing that Sheila was a skillful cosmetician, Darcy didn't have enough nerve to ask Constance to do hers.

With her skin cooled by the wet cloth, she applied foundation, dabbing her face with unsteady hands and smoothing creamy makeup into her hairline and down her neck. She remembered to put touches of brownish red under her eyebrows, on her cheeks, and below the outer corners of her eyes, but the array of blending powders stumped her. Staring helplessly at the clutter of creams, cakes, powders, tubes, and sticks, she picked up an eyebrow pencil and emphasized her fine brows, then noticed that Constance was using black grease on the tip of an orange stick to apply light feathery strokes.

Darcy was still too pale for stage lighting, but her own ghostlike image reminded her to mix deep red with a touch of dark green in her palm and blend the mixture down each side of her face and under her cheekbones. One of the apprentices, an authority on makeup, had told her to use a dark mixture of red and blue across her eyelids, using her fingertips to blend the unlikely combination. With a fine brush she also drew black cream lines below her lower lashes and over the upper ones, thickening them with several layers of brownish-black mascara. Absorption in her task was helping her nerves as she colored her lips with carmine and dotted a bit in the inner corner of each eye. Dusting the whole job lightly with powder, she approved of the slight narrowing of her face and the healthy glow.

Making up her mind to be ready for the part wasn't quite so efficiently done. With hair coiled over her ears at Nick's insistence, she felt old and jaded, not young and innocent like Beth. No matter how hard she concentrated, she still imagined Sheila in the audience, her head smothered in some ridiculous blond wig. Ken absolutely forbade anyone opening the curtains to the entrance ramp even an inch before a performance, but rules or no rules, she had to look at the audience. No one was near, so she gingerly parted the heavy woven cloth that substituted for a door to hide the work area, peering out at the people finding their seats.

A sharp slap on her bottom made her swing around sputtering, coming face to face with Nick.

"Be professional!" he hissed. "You're not the star of the senior class play anymore."

"That hurt!" She rubbed the spot.

"I owe you more than that for our weekend in Buffalo. Get into character now, and forget about the audience."

He was right; she had to concentrate. Finding a shadowy corner where she could wait alone, she forced herself to think all the thoughts Beth might have in her head. With a tremendous effort of will, she stopped hearing everything around her, knowing that one of the keys to Beth's personality was the isolation imposed by silence. She was still frightened of moving up that ramp, guided only by pilots, the low blue lights that allowed actors and crews to move and work on darkened stages. She was terrified of being alone under the spotlight in her first scene and sure she'd be hopelessly awkward and unresponsive.

In one way, Darcy thought, she was like Beth: she'd never felt more alone in her life.

Nick was beside her, materializing like a ghost. She hadn't heard him approach, but she saw that he was David. He'd slipped into his part just as he'd demanded that she become Beth before going onstage. When he lifted her hand to his lips and kissed the tip of her little finger, it was David trying to communicate his love to Beth. She was ready to begin the play.

A stage surrounded by an audience is a different world; consciously realizing it, Darcy was energized by it. All the gestures and moves that had become automatic through rehearsing now became natural. She was Beth, thinking Beth's thoughts and reacting as Beth would. It was like making love, climbing to a peak that surpassed all other highs.

Exiting down the ramp before the house lights came on for intermission, Darcy couldn't quite believe what had happened. Her legs were trembling, and she felt like a swimmer surfacing after staying underwater to the limits of her ability.

"Keep it up, darling!" Nick hurried past her, patting her shoulder.

An intermission that seemed long to the audience hardly existed for the players. Ken was the nucleus of an exploding galaxy, the only one who seemed to see the whole scene. There was a set change with hurried switching of props, and the dressing rooms were chaotic as players scrambled to dress for the second act. This play had a small cast and simple sets. Darcy couldn't imagine what it must be like between acts during a big musical.

Gradually, Constance's calmness registered on Darcy, and she realized that most of the frantic scurrying was in her imagination. The backstage crew was wonderfully efficient, knowing their jobs and doing them rapidly and confidently.

She wanted to splash her face with icy water, but there wasn't time to redo her makeup. Settling for a glass of water, she changed into the pink skirt she'd fought to wear and patted her makeup with a powder puff to take the shine off her face. Her skin seemed to be soaking up the heavy grease-paint, but there was no time to worry about it.

Act II was beginning. With less time to psych herself into the role, Darcy had to concentrate even harder. At first she felt stiff, aware of the audience all around her, but the smooth professionalism of the other players pulled her through the first awkward minutes. She was Beth again, struggling for a firm hold on her own life.

In the last scene she cried. Tears weren't part of the role as she'd rehearsed it, but they belonged in the scene. Beth's bittersweet decision meant even more because Darcy genuinely shared her pain.

Applause resounded from all sides, and Nick held her hand for the curtain call, whispering, "You deserve this."

Backstage the crew and cast were congratulating each other, excited because the first show of the season had been so well-received. No modern-day thespian would admit it, but theatrical people are superstitious, looking for omens with secret fervor, reading the success of a show in a complicated set of signs and portents. Tonight they loved Darcy; she was their good luck charm, their long shot who came in first. Darcy found their approval intoxicating. No wonder Sheila was so committed to the life of a performer! she thought.

Sheila! She'd actually forgotten her sister was in the audience!

"A woman left this for you at the box office," Ken said, handing her a note written on a folded bank deposit slip.

Her sister's message was short and blunt: orders to come to a motel in Traverse City. There was no word of congratulations for performing the part so well. Sheila assumed Darcy would be willing to drive and meet her late at night after an exhausting performance. She even included a sketchy map showing where she was staying.

Like her infrequent letters, this note was uniquely Sheila, spelling out what she wanted with a minimum of words:

Darcy folded and refolded it, making a wad of the paper. She could find the motel without any trouble, but her twin was being unfair. Certainly anything they had to say could wait until morning.

The other women, more experienced at quick changes and removing makeup, left the dressing room before Darcy, leaving her alone in front of the square mirror illuminated by a bright tube of light.

"Alone?" Nick parted the curtains that served as a door.

"Yes. I'm the slow one."

"I'm glad." He bent over her and kissed the back of her neck, releasing her hair from the buns over her ears and letting it cascade down her shoulders. "It'll take me a little while to finish here," he said, drawing the key to his cabin from his pants pocket and placing it in front of her.

"Nick, I—"

"No." He covered her lips with his fingers. "Take this spare key and wait for me in my cabin. We'll talk then."

The key was so ordinary, its gold-colored surface tarnished and worn with age. Who would believe a little bit of metal could generate such indecision and longing? How much loyalty did she owe Sheila, and what did she owe herself? With an intensity foreign to her nature, she wanted to go to Nick and lie in his arms. Depriving herself of one last chance to be with him would be sheer torture. Her sister was asking too much; she had to be with Nick tonight.

She hurried to her own cabin first, showering with scented honeysuckle soap until the smell of cold cream was only a memory. After powdering herself generously, she slipped into a simple dusty rose dress, the jersey clinging to her bare body. Thrusting her feet into her high heels, she locked the door behind her, putting Sheila completely out of her mind.

Nick had hurried too. When she eased open the door, he was standing beside the dresser, splashing cologne on his cheeks, a dark brown towel wrapped around his hips. Darcy closed and bolted the door, knowing she wasn't there to talk.

His smile was beautiful, starting at his eyes and transforming his whole face. She loved him without reservation, cherishing his glow of happiness and the welcome in his arms. Whatever he'd planned to say was forgotten.

Prolonging the anticipation, she left his arms and walked to the edge of the bed, covered like hers with a coarsely woven cotton spread, and sat on the edge, crossing her legs. She'd never played the part of a seductress before; in real life lovemaking had always seemed a trifle frightening to her. But tonight she was an actress, putting body and heart into the most important scene of her life. Tomorrow Sheila would demand to step into the role at the Duckeye; tonight was Darcy's. Even if Nick never spoke to her again, he'd remember that for one night she'd loved him without reservation.

"Sheila." He played with the name on his tongue, spreading it out like a mystical password.

"Your cabin is larger." Her face was telling him far more than her words. "And your bed is nicer."

She stretched out on her side, pushing off her shoes with her toes, letting the clinging jersey ride up her thigh and drape the enticing curve of her hip. Her breasts were straining against the bodice, and she unbottoned first one button and then another, continuing until her dress was open to the waist.

Nick watched intently, a small grin playing at the corners of his lips, but he didn't move.

Being a sultry siren wasn't an easy job! She certainly had his attention, but he showed no signs of coming to her. She wasn't at all sure what to do next.

"You look comfortable." He tightened the towel at his waist and watched her with amusement.

"Sit by me." She shifted her hips and patted the bed beside her.

"I have a feeling we can talk better if I stay right here."

"I'm lonesome here alone."

Was she getting too corny? It had never occurred to her that he wouldn't cooperate!

"I'll be lonesome for the rest of the summer if you don't stay," he said.

"What if I have a really good reason for going? Would you want to see me later?"

"When I'm casting the play in New York?"

"Nick, that has nothing to do with the way I feel about you." She sat up, forgetting about her open bodice, and walked to where he stood.

"How do you feel about me?" His words were cool, but his eyes were hungry, watching the swell of her breasts barely covered by the parted cloth.

"I love you." There was a catch in her voice, and the words came from the depths of her soul.

"You said that line so well, darling." He sounded deeply sad. "I wish I could believe it."

"You can. I do love you, Nick." She stood tiptoe to press her mouth against his, circling his waist with arms strengthened by yearning, clinging to him as though she expected to be thrown aside.

"Sheila, you don't know how desperately I want to believe you this time." He let his hand slide over her back, discovering for himself that the dress was the only garment she wore.

"Please believe me!" She'd wither away if he didn't kiss her.

"Say you'll stay. It could be the beginning of something wonderful." Her dress was slippery under his caresses, and he inched the skirt upward, sliding his hands over the smooth, bare indentation at the base of her spine.

"Let something wonderful happen now." She found the edge of his towel, loosening it so the thick terry cloth fell to a heap at his feet.

"You're going to make me fight for my virtue." His voice was husky with passion, and he slowly took her lips, lightly sampling their sweetness as his arms encircled her.

"Do you want to fight me?" Fear of rejection made her voice quiver.

"You know I don't." He gave in to his own blinding desires, letting his hands roam over her breasts, pushing the dress from her shoulders to reveal downy-soft mounds with hard, blushing nipples, then easing the soft cloth over her hips to fall to her ankles.

"You're the only woman I know whose nipples change color," he murmured, kissing her now with more abandon, scooping her into his arms and carrying her to the bed.

"Love me," she begged desperately, wanting to be wholly his before her deception came tumbling down on her head. "Love me, Nick."

He leaned over her, memorizing her beautiful face with the tip of his finger. His eyes burned with need, but he held back, studying her with his body held stiffly apart from hers.

"The princess bestowing her favors?" he asked with a trace of sarcasm that lashed at her conscience.

"No."

"If I hadn't seen your performance tonight, I wouldn't believe you could act this well. Do you really want me so much, darling?"

"I love you," she cried, pulling his head to her breast, cradling it, stroking his neck and shoulders until she felt an answering shudder. "Oh, Nick, I love you."

"I want to believe that!" He straightened beside her, holding her in his arms until their hearts seemed to pound in unison.

His kisses seared her eyelids and put blossoms on her cheeks, filling her with warmth and desire. Feeling his tongue in her ear and on the hollow of her throat made her want him with every fiber of her being, but for long, agonizing minutes she knew he was holding back, suspicious and uncommitted, weighing the risks of giving himself completely.

138

"I love you," she murmured, not caring that tears filled her eyes and made her sniffle.

She went limp in his arms, clinging and docile, not wanting to play the seductress anymore.

"Where do you fit into my life?" he asked in a hoarse whisper, holding her so close that the heat of his body flowed through her.

"I don't know."

The walls were pale green and the ceiling was white, but where they met, a careless painter had let the colors run together. It was the last thing she noticed about the cabin that night.

The open window over the bed fanned them with air as warm as a dragon's breath, heavy with moisture and saturated with the scent of forest and lake. Their bodies were slippery, gleaming with health and vigorous strength. His caresses were almost unbearably pleasurable, and she found delight in the muscular leanness of his limbs and the tautness of his stomach. Exploring his rib cage, she planted tiny kisses near his navel, marveling at his readiness for love.

Their lovemaking became a romp and then a joust, a contest to determine who could give more joy to the other. At last able to shed all her inhibitions like a second skin, she knew that learning to play Beth had made her more caring and giving. Living in another mind, even for such a short time, made her own love blossom. The depth of her feelings grew, and she wanted to share her most private, secretive self with this man she loved.

No wonder she'd never really loved before! Only Nick could touch her heart.

With pink and swollen lips she followed the firm contours of his shoulders and back, loving the ripples of muscle and the golden tanned skin. How could she go back to her former life after having known Nick's love? How could one night satisfy her hunger for this man, a hunger she knew would endure for the rest of her life?

They dozed and woke again, coming together because it was intolerable to have even an inch of space separating them. He quoted lines of love to her from every play in his memory and she responded with kisses and intimate smiles. The night was magical. If they weren't in love, Darcy thought, then day was night and truth was a sham.

Reality returned with the dawn, and although he loved her with a return of the evening's fervor, she was already stricken by the pain of separation. When he swelled within her, she felt sore, making him worry that he'd loved her too much, or too roughly. Brushing aside his concern, she tried to lose herself in his arms one more time, but reality kept intruding.

In a few short hours she had to face her sister. Was she strong enough to send Sheila away, to usurp her place forever in the arms of her lover? Even as Nick teased her for being a lazy riser, slow to awake and sluggish to respond, Darcy was dreading the day to come. Her sense of fairness told her Sheila had a right to be in the play. The contract was in her name; her talent had earned her the opportunity to be there. She had foolishly agreed to take Sheila's place, but she still had no right to the part in *Wings of Love*.

"Are you still with me?" Nick whispered, moving his lips over her lowered lids.

Moments earlier he'd been euphoric, satiated but so much in love that new yearnings stole over him at the sight of his beloved, her raven hair tousled on the pillow and her nipples as pink as her lips, both inviting him to savor their sweetness again.

She mumbled a noncommital answer and snuggled closer, drinking in the raw but exciting scent of his skin and the rough hairiness of his leg against hers.

"Sheila, don't pretend you're going back to sleep, or I'll throw you in a cold shower." He buried his face against her midriff and made a grumbling sound. She hugged his head, disappointed when he sat up and looked into her eyes.

"We were meant to be together, you know. It's kismet, fate. It's written in the stars. You can't argue with your own destiny, darling."

"Do you see a warm shower in my future?" She attempted to joke, but he wasn't having any of it.

He gave her a love squeeze on a convenient part of her anatomy, then leaned so close all she could see were his eyes, heavenly blue with lashes almost sinfully long on a rugged-looking man.

"You're not leaving this bed until you agree to stay here the rest of the summer."

"Doesn't this state have a law against holding hostages?"

"You're on my ship, mate, and I make the laws."

"You're not my captain!"

"No? I should make you walk the plank for insubordination."

"Only pirates do that!"

"You're the pirate! You've shanghaied my heart."

"You should write messages for valentine greetings."

"Why do I feel that you're still trying to avoid the issue?" He pinned her down with one strong leg and arm.

"Maybe because I am." She was sinking into a depth of misery that should have been impossible lying beside the man she fervently loved.

If Sheila took her place now, Darcy thought, she would gladly stay all summer just to be in Nick's new play. In her own way Sheila would be grateful for the opportunity, but Darcy couldn't bear the pain. Tomorrow night it could be her sister lying in Nick's arms, basking in his love.

Turning aside suddenly, she buried her face in the pillow, summoning the resolve to tell Nick the worst lie of her life.

"Darling, what's wrong?" The concern in his voice lashed her more painfully than a whip.

"We can't do this again." She forced the words out of her throat, not daring to look at him.

"What can't we do again?" His voice was icy.

"This." She tried to crawl away but his hands had an iron grip on her arms, forcing her to face him.

"Are you telling me you won't stay the summer?"

"Yes. And this is the last time I can sleep with you."

"That doesn't make sense!"

She shook her head, numb with pain.

"You didn't sleep with me to further your career. You couldn't have been pretending you loved me last night. I know it meant as much to you as it did to me. You were warm and loving. . . ."

His pain and disappointment were torturing her, striking her dumb when she most needed to tell him the truth.

"Damn it, Sheila! You can't get away with leaving me again. What did you hope to gain by misleading me?"

Shaking convulsively, she had to escape. Moving to the edge of the bed, she saw her shoes on the floor and poked her feet into them, too stunned to care if she looked ridiculous wearing nothing but heels. Where was her dress?

Her face was red and wet from the river of tears beating silently down her cheeks before she found her dress where Nick had placed it, on a chair beside his towel. Struggling into it, she found her own cabin key and escaped through the door, sure that nothing worse could ever happen to her.

Much later, exhausted from sobbing but still screaming and crying inside, she took a hasty shower and changed into slacks and a white top, steeling herself for one more ordeal: her meeting with her sister.

142

CHAPTER EIGHT

"Where were you last night?" Sheila sounded frantic, hugging Darcy with spontaneous affection. "I was scared to death when you didn't come. I called the playhouse, and some man went to your cabin. He said you didn't answer the door but your car was still there, so at least I knew you hadn't had an accident driving here."

"I'm sorry you were worried." Darcy certainly hadn't expected to find her twin so anxious about her safety.

"Worried! I was petrified!" Sheila gave her another hug. "If anything happened to you after you came here for me . . ."

"Nothing did," Darcy forced herself to say, knowing very well that meeting Nick at the Duckeye was the worst catastrophe of her life.

"Well, you're here, so everything is okay. I'm sorry about this room; it was all I could find on such short notice."

Darcy looked around without interest at the somewhat shabby motel room.

"It's no worse than the cabins at the Duckeye."

"I imagine not. I've just about had it with summer stock —hard-water showers and breakfast at seven, just like summer camp."

Darcy remembered another of her lies to Nick: Sheila had never been a camp counselor. One summer at Girl Scout camp had been enough to last her sister a lifetime.

"I'll have to go back there with your car," Sheila said,

sounding businesslike as she outlined her plan to take her rightful place at the theater. "I reserved this room for the week, and you can use the car I rented. I'll pay for all of it out of my share of the Duckeye contract. You can just enjoy yourself, go to the beach, do whatever summer people do here."

"You expect me to stay here until the play closes?"

"I suppose I could drive your car back to Springfield. I did promise to visit Mom and Dad. But you've got to stay a day or two. There's so much you have to tell me. I need to know where your costumes are and what makeup you've been using and—"

"That's why you want me to stay?" Darcy looked mournfully at her sister; wasn't she going to say anything about the way she'd played Beth?

"You can't just leave without telling me everything that's happened!"

"Did you like the show?"

"You did an adequate job, you really did, Darcy."

"Adequate?"

Darcy had gone to meet her sister expecting to feel angry with her. Instead she felt sad, inexpressively heavy-hearted. It would never occur to Sheila that anything about the summer theater was important to her sister.

"All right, you were good, very good," Sheila said begrudgingly. "I told you, you know a lot more about deaf people than I do."

"Let me finish the play, Sheila."

"I can't do that! Why on earth would you want to? You don't want an acting career now, do you?"

"No, I only want to finish this play."

"That's crazy! What good would it do you?"

"I've made something of the part. I want the satisfaction of finishing it."

"Oh, Darcy, anyone can stand around and play dumb! I have to get out to the Duckeye. Nicholas Cross is my best

144

chance for a Broadway role. You can't expect me to go back to New York without something lined up for the fall."

"He won't give you a part."

"How can you know that?" Sheila was pacing, so agitated she didn't need to put on a performance for her sister's benefit.

"He won't let you use him."

"Have you done something to make him angry?"

"Have I done something? Sheila, you left him without a word. How can you expect him to forget that?"

"Oh, men have short memories. Unless there's something you're not telling me."

"Let's talk about all the things you haven't told me! Does Nick know you have a twin?"

"Of course not! I never tell anyone. Do you want to run to New York so we can do some silly commercial with twins on a tandem bicycle brushing with different toothpastes?"

Darcy knew that having a separate identity was important to her sister; she hadn't suspected that Sheila concealed her twin's existence, reducing her to the status of a skeleton in the family closet.

"Let me finish the play, Sheila," Darcy begged.

"No, you don't know what you're asking!"

"I do, but *Wings of Love* doesn't mean a thing to you. Nick will never give you a part. I know it."

"There is something you're not telling me." Sheila sat on the edge of the bed, crossing her ankles and looking at Darcy. "You don't have a crush on Nick, do you? It's an occupational hazard of working with him."

"I love him."

"Oh, Darcy, be serious! You can't expect anything to come of it! If Nick seems interested in you, it's because he believes you're me."

Darcy took a deep breath, clenching her fists to forget the pain in her heart. She didn't want to believe her sister was right. When she first arrived at the Duckeye, Nick made it

145

clear that he no longer loved Sheila. But what else would he say to a woman who had ruthlessly left him without a word of good-bye?

"I'm going to take over the part," Sheila said grimly. "There's no point in trying to dissuade me. You have nothing to gain by finishing the play, unless there's more between you and Nick than you've told me."

"He's very angry at me."

"At me, you mean! What did you do to make him mad?"

"I refused to stay the rest of the summer with him."

"Is that all?" Sheila laughed with relief. "I'll just go tell him I've changed my mind."

"No!"

"Darcy, you'll get over this infatuation. You always did get interested in my boyfriends."

"You don't really care about Nick!"

"Of course I do. He's handsome, successful, and one of Broadway's most promising directors."

"I'm not going to let you do the play!"

"Be reasonable, Darcy. You've done a tremendous favor for me, and I'm grateful, really I am. But I'm not going to starve and pound the pavements auditioning when I can persuade Nick to give me a little part in his new play."

"He won't."

"I think he will, if I agree to stay the rest of the summer."

"If he sees two of us—"

"He'll be angry with you. You're the fraud. I'll explain that I couldn't get to rehearsals, so you took my place. How could I know you wouldn't tell him who you were? I have a contract; he has to let me do the play."

"This means more to me than I can explain," Darcy said miserably, feeling her resistance wither like cut flowers abandoned in the sun.

"To me too," Sheila insisted. "I'm going out to the Duck-eye. I'll drive the rental car. I can always say that yours is

146

being repaired. I'll need the cabin key, unless you want me to report it lost."

"I can't believe you're doing this!"

Darcy hated herself, not her sister. It was her own fault for agreeing to the whole deception in the first place, and what did she have to gain by going back to the Duckeye? Nick would despise her for pretending to be Sheila. Even if he could forgive her for stepping into the role of Beth, he'd never understand why she encouraged him to fall in love with her.

"Wear my clothes home," Sheila offered magnanimously. "I'll see that you get your things back after the play, if you'll do the same with mine. I assume you are going home, since you don't seem willing to help me."

Darcy didn't answer.

"I have enough cash to cover the motel bill for last night." She counted out some money and laid it on a dresser top. "When the Duckeye pays me, I'll split it half and half with you. I wish you wouldn't sit there looking as if I've just broken your favorite toy."

"We're not children anymore." Resentment made Darcy's words sharper than she'd intended.

"No, well, what can I say? I am terribly grateful, but I don't understand what you could possibly gain by going back to the Duckeye. You're just not making sense, Darcy."

"Love doesn't make sense." She saw that Sheila seemed not to hear this.

"I'll just take my makeup bag. Oh, and I might want this." She pulled a sheer black nightgown from an open suitcase, shaking it out and refolding it before putting it in her big straw bag.

Darcy bit her lower lip, feeling more helpless and frustrated than she ever had in her life. Nothing she could say to Sheila would stop her from going to the Duckeye, and to Nick.

"I don't suppose you want to tell me what you and Nick

147

have been doing?" Sheila asked without any expectation of a reply. "Well, men are all the same, only Nick is cuter than most."

She left, leaving the scent of her sultry perfume in the air and a void in Darcy's heart. Putting a DO NOT DISTURB sign on the door and lying down on bed linens still smelling sweetly of her sister's night cream and cologne, Darcy fell asleep because thinking was unbearable.

Her mother always said that things looked better after a good sleep but she was wrong, Darcy thought, waking to a gray world, not realizing for several minutes that an overcast sky had drained the color from the room. Her first instinct was to leave for home immediately, to put hundreds of miles between herself and the heartache and disappointment of the Duckeye Playhouse.

Her clothes were hopelessly wrinkled from sleeping in them, but rummaging through Sheila's luggage for a fresh outfit was unthinkable. Her mind felt dull and hazy. She left the room, putting the motel key in her purse, and noticed that Sheila hadn't taken the cabin key.

A nondescript little coffee shop was attached to the motel, and Darcy was ravenous, desperate to replenish spent energy. She ordered the dinner special of Swiss steak and mashed potatoes with a salad and ate without tasting the food, hardly aware that it was after four o'clock in the afternoon.

Stopping at the desk, she confirmed that Sheila had booked the room for a week. Too listless to change the reservation, she decided to tell the clerk later that one more night would be enough.

Without any enthusiasm she located a cute little women's wear shop stocked with fashionable casual clothing for the prosperous summer trade. Using her credit card, Darcy bought a crisp navy skirt and two sleeveless cotton blouses, one with a sailor collar and the other with a cool pink flowered pattern. With some new underwear, she thought, she could get home without exploring the contents of her sister's several suitcases and garment bag. There had to be a way to have her luggage delivered to the playhouse. Sheila could explain the presence of extra baggage just as glibly as she would that of a rented car.

Lethargic and apathetic, sensing that control of her own fate had slipped from her hands, Darcy returned to the motel room, spending the evening in front of a TV until hunger drove her out for a sandwich at the same coffee shop just before it closed for the night. She took a cold roast beef sandwich and a chocolate milk shake back to her room, devouring every speck and still feeling empty. She went to bed, surprised that misery was making her dead-tired as well as gluttonous.

The sun woke her; it was eight-thirty, late to begin the long drive home. The only sensible thing to do, was call ahead for motel reservations at some halfway point. She thought of going to her car to check the road map in the glove compartment, but another idea was nagging at her consciousness: Could Sheila play the part of Beth as well as she had? Her emotions were numb where her sister was concerned, but being able to succeed in the role of the deaf girl had left a residue of happiness in her. Denying to herself that Nick had any part in her urge to see a performance of *Wings of Love,* she showered and dressed, waiting until nine to call the ticket office. The production was nearly sold out for the whole run, but the apprentice who answered did locate a single seat left in a row booked by a large group.

The actors on stage wouldn't notice a lone woman in the audience, but some of the apprentices who served as ticket takers and ushers might recognize her or be puzzled because she was a double of the actress starring in the play. She searched Sheila's suitcases, finding the blond wig in a plastic bag beside a hair dryer. The artificial hair was silvery blond, sleek against her head and turning up in a jaunty curl just below the ears. Darcy thought she looked silly, but only

149

someone who knew her well would recognize her. With sunglasses she could remove after the play started, she wouldn't be recognized. The audience and backstage areas of the theater were worlds apart.

The day was sunny and warm; she drove, then wandered on foot, enjoying the venerable old resort town and the impressive homes, many of them built years ago as summer residences for wealthy families from Chicago and other urban centers. She fell in love with a yellow Victorian house dripping with gingerbread trim and flanked by a wide porch furnished with white wicker.

Grand Traverse Bay was a cold, violet-blue, shimmering under the glare of the sun, but she wasn't in the mood to try finding a bathing beach. She wandered in and out of specialty shops, which held her attention for a few hours, but the lovely resort area was wasted on her. She looked around as a tourist would, but nothing could distract her from the turmoil in her mind. She had to force herself not to leave too early for the theater; the drive took less than an hour, and she didn't want to be the first one there.

The wig made her hot, and she felt anything but jaunty in the crisp navy-trimmed white sailor's blouse. Sheila's luggage was in the back of the car; Darcy planned to return to the motel following the performance and after she'd found a way to get rid of her sister's possessions, maybe by paying an usher to deliver them to the cabin. Then there wouldn't be anything to keep her in Michigan another day.

Her timing was good; cars were streaming into the bumpy mowed field that served as a parking area. She maneuvered her car between two white posts, the reflectors not needed as the long summer daylight still illuminated the lakeside site. Seeing the barn as a theatergoer, she was impressed by the spruce rustic setting, excited in spite of her nervousness.

She delayed, leaving her sunglasses on, sipping a cola she'd bought at an outdoor stand sheltered by a huge red-and-white striped umbrella, making sure most of the audi-

150

ence was seated before she went inside. Sheila's picture, glamorous with makeup that made her eyes seem larger, taunted her from the display case, and Darcy felt a cleansing stab of anger. She'd been blaming herself, flogging her conscience; using her sister as a target for some of her anger was probably a healthy thing to do.

To reach her seat she had to slide past a row of men dressed in pastel linen jackets and women in sleeveless and strapless silk and jersey gowns, summer people who wore their wealth and position with easy grace. An admiring glance from several of the men did nothing to make her feel less alone.

Nick, in the part of David, seemed younger than she knew him to be; he moved with a fluid ease, using his body as a youth would without seeming awkward or gauche. When he spoke, his voice had a resonance that sent chills down her spine, and she wondered if anyone had ever died of love.

At first she could only see Nick; even when he wasn't on the stage, her mind followed him, dwelling on the way she felt about him. Then she started watching Sheila, and the feeling that something was wrong grew. In the park bench scene her sister reacted to Nick's voice behind her, a bad blunder for someone playing the part of a deaf person. Sheila was wearing a different costume, a short red skirt that revealed attractive legs but was jarringly out of character. Had Nick or Fran okayed the change? Darcy very much doubted it.

During intermission she blended in with the crowd smoking and buying cups of soda outside the theater, but her mind stayed on the performance. What effect was it having on the audience? Wandering slowly, she picked up snatches of conversation. The story had impact. The cast was strong, but something was missing: the deaf girl's struggles just weren't convincing.

Darcy had never known Sheila to fail in a role, and she hadn't come hoping to see her sister humiliated. She just

151

wanted to be sure the play was all right in her absence, but so far what she'd seen was distressing.

The second act was worse. For one thing, Sheila was faking the sign language. Instead of making the gesture for please, open hand on her chest with the palm inward, rubbing in small circles, she just flapped her fingers. Enough signs were done correctly to thoroughly confuse anyone who knew the language of the deaf, but whenever memory failed her, she made convulsive little wiggles with her fingers that were totally meaningless.

The audience might have overlooked this lapse but they couldn't miss the brittle smile on Sheila's face when she should have registered more complex feelings. She was making Beth into a nice but shallow person, incapable of expressing deep feelings or anxiety about the future. Either Sheila had completely misunderstood the character, or she didn't have enough sensitivity to generate sympathy.

The other players were aware of what was happening; they worked heroically to save the play, but without a warm, real Beth, they were severely handicapped. In the last scene, Darcy felt relieved that David wasn't tying himself to the undeserving deaf woman, which wasn't at all the feeling the play was supposed to leave with the audience. Sheila was totally wrong for the part; without clever lines to deliver and attention-getting humorous scenes, she didn't seem to have any interest in the role.

Forgetting the luggage in the back of her car, Darcy drove back to the motel in a turmoil over the way Sheila was ruining the part, *her* part. Tomorrow was Sunday, with an early curtain scheduled. Monday the theater was dark. She couldn't bear to see her sister's performance again, but leaving things as they were was impossible. Instead of departing for home Sunday, she spent a long, restless day, walking for miles, trying to decide what, if anything, she should do.

Early Monday morning she checked out of the motel and drove toward the Duckeye, stopping to put on the tight, hot wig a few miles from the theater. With no performance that day, it was almost certain that Sheila would still be sleeping, but Darcy couldn't drive her car onto the grounds. The last thing she wanted was to be seen in a car that was supposed to belong to her sister.

Following the road that circled the lake, she had no difficulty locating a turnoff where she could safely park her car. The walk back to the theater wasn't long for a person who loved hiking, but it was agonizing in Darcy's state of mind. With no makeup and large, dark sunglasses, she wasn't too worried about being recognized, but a confrontation with Sheila might be a disaster. What could she say to her stubborn sister? Did Sheila have any idea of what she was doing to the play? Would she believe that Darcy cared about the role of Beth enough to come there? Knowing Sheila, she expected a stormy scene with threats and accusations.

Activity on the musical, which opened as soon as *Wings of Love* closed, made the playhouse a beehive of activity, but Darcy passed the theater without being challenged; everyone was too busy to pay any attention to a stranger.

Her real fears crystallized as she approached cabin six. Would she find Sheila there alone? Or would her sister be in Nick's cabin, still dozing in the bed she'd shared with him? Darcy was trembling, her legs unsteady and her palms damp as she tentatively tapped on the door. Getting no response, she knocked more forcefully, repeating her summons until her knuckles hurt.

There was no real reason to knock; she still had a key. The worst that could happen was that she'd find Nick inside with her sister, but he wouldn't sleep late on a day when so much was being done to prepare for the musical. She inserted her key and slowly pushed the door inward.

Sheila was in bed, groggily pulling herself into a sitting position.

"What are you doing here?" She pushed aside tangled

hair. "Are you crazy, coming to my cabin in broad daylight?"

"No one noticed me." Darcy shut the door behind her.

"I thought you were going home." Sheila yawned, frowning deeply and making no effort to leave the bed.

"I was. I decided to see the play first."

"You went to a performance? When?"

"Saturday night."

"Then why didn't you leave yesterday? You're certainly not helping me any by hanging around. I've had nothing but trouble with that wardrobe hag, and I don't even know her name. If I'd known you were staying, you could've told me a few of the things I need to know. You can't imagine what a strain the last two days have been."

"I can imagine."

There was no sympathy in Darcy's voice; she realized that her sister didn't really care why she'd come. To her it was only a minor annoyance to have to wake up and deal with her twin.

"Where's your car?" Sheila asked.

"On the lake road. No one will see it."

"Well, why are you here?" Sheila slid her feet to the floor and stretched; she was wearing Darcy's yellow cotton nightgown, not the slinky black one she'd taken with her.

"I want to finish the play myself," Darcy said firmly.

"You are stagestruck!" Sheila grinned with a trace of mockery.

"No."

"You want another chance with Nick," Sheila accused her in a cold voice.

Darcy didn't bother to deny this. She didn't want to tell her sister she was ruining the play, preferring to let her believe whatever she liked.

"You can't deny I did well in the play. I want to finish the run."

"What do you like about that dreary little play? I've never

been in anything so boring. All I do is stand around and look dumb!"

"Yes, that is all you do. You shouldn't mind letting me do it for you."

"Why? I don't understand why." Sheila did a few lazy stretching exercises, then examined her face in the dresser mirror, staring intently at a tiny mark only she could see.

Her sister was stalling, trying to manipulate her as she always had. Darcy saw this so clearly that it brought tears to her eyes. Her twin didn't care why she wanted to play Beth in the remaining performances. She was only weighing the advantages and disadvantages to herself.

"The part is very important to me," Darcy said softly.

"Nick is very important to you, you mean. Well, he's impossible! He'll barely speak to me! I asked him casually about his new play, and he nearly bit my head off! Whatever happened between you two, it's ruining my chances. I've never seen him so hostile! The only time he talks to me is to criticize the way I'm doing that dopey part. He can't understand why I've fallen apart after opening night!"

"Then why stay here?" Darcy asked.

Nick had every right to hate her, but at least she'd made him immune to Sheila.

"Oh, I can't think before I have my morning shower."

She flounced into the bathroom, running the shower while Darcy paced in suspenseful agony. Returning with a towel tied around her and her hair clinging like a black cap on her head, Sheila stood in front of the dresser mirror brushing her hair and ignoring her sister.

How can she look so much like me and be so different? Darcy wondered unhappily, wanting to love her sister as she always had but finding it increasingly difficult. What did Sheila really want from life? Was the momentary applause of an audience her only reward from the theater?

"You're still here," Sheila said without looking at her.

"Yes." Darcy couldn't imagine why Sheila would expect her to leave without settling anything.

"Now, what is this about you doing my part?"

She dropped the towel to the floor and stepped over it, rummaging in a dresser drawer for a pair of panties. Darcy averted her eyes, uncomfortable for the first time in her life with her twin's nudity. Maybe her sister's body, so much like hers but getting a little heavier in the rear and thighs, made her realize that they were no longer intimately connected; their lives were going in different directions, and neither of them had any real desire to salvage their former closeness. For Darcy it was a revelation; she suspected that Sheila had always rebelled against their sameness, using it only when it suited her purposes.

Darcy felt a sense of loss, an estrangement from the person who had been closest to her throughout her formative years. With a heavy sigh, she knew she had to let Sheila go her own way. There was relief as well as sorrow in the decision.

"You can have the whole salary for the engagement. I just want to be Beth until the play closes."

"Darcy, that's crazy!" She bent over to snap a pink bra, then slipped into her sister's favorite white shorts. "You certainly didn't bring many clothes."

"Yours are in the car." She groped for words to convince her sister to switch again without telling her how terrible she was in the part.

"Give me one good reason why you should take over."

"Your sign language. You've forgotten most of it."

"Oh." Sheila made a gesture of dismissal. "Who knows the difference?"

"Anyone in the audience who knows sign language."

"One or two people during the whole run maybe. What's your real reason, Darcy? Nick?"

"No." She was afraid of facing him again. "I can do the part better."

156

Sheila started brushing her hair again, giving herself moments to weigh Darcy's claim.

"Well, I'm not having any fun with it, I can tell you that. That teacher—what's her name?"

"Constance."

"She's such a know-it-all, I could scream. How can I do scenes with someone who keeps giving me helpful hints?"

"She helped me immensely. I couldn't have gotten into the part without her."

"And Nick is impossible! I'd rather do a love scene with the Sphinx!"

"He's angry, but it didn't show in his performance Saturday."

"Well, I'm used to a more professional cast."

"Cole Handley was acting before you were born."

"He's an egotistical bore."

"And you don't like the apprentices either?"

"I really didn't notice them one way or another."

"You know the play isn't going well. Do you really think it's everyone's fault but yours?"

"For goodness sake, Darcy, you sound more like Mother all the time. What do you want from me?"

"I want you to leave and let me finish the play."

"I don't want to!"

"Why?"

"There's still a chance that Nick will thaw. I've seen the way he stares at me when he thinks I'm not looking. I know it's a long shot, but he's still my best prospect."

"No, he's not." Darcy shook her head sadly, reluctant to threaten her sister but sure Sheila would never leave just to be fair and kind. "I'm staying, Sheila. If you stay, there will be two of us here."

"Are you saying you'll let Nick know about the switch?"

"I won't need to if he sees both of us together. He'll ask his own questions."

"That's a dirty trick, Darcy!"

157

"I'm not proud of anything I've done lately, except playing Beth."

"I don't believe you! You've never had the slightest interest in acting. Why now, all of a sudden, do you decide you have to have a part? You're doing it just to interfere in my life!" Sheila's voice was harsh with anger.

"I love you," Darcy said truthfully, "but playing the part is terribly important to me. I don't think I'm hurting you by doing it."

"You're certainly annoying me!"

Surprising herself, Darcy laughed, going to her sister and hugging her, a farewell gesture. "You'll be all right. The Duckeye check will last until you find something. You're sure to get some commercials when you get back to New York."

"You really expect me to go quietly?"

Darcy only nodded.

"I want my own clothes."

"We'll drive the rental out to where I'm parked and switch them."

"Nick has been beastly! I'll be glad to get away from him. He has a temper, you know. Once I got so mad I slapped him, and you wouldn't believe what he threatened to do."

"I'll be sure not to make him mad."

"I never lived with him, if that's what you're thinking." Sheila was shoving cosmetics into her flowered bag.

"I don't want to hear about it."

"I suppose it doesn't matter. He won't be any nicer to you than he has been to me."

"Are you ready to leave?" Being with her twin was becoming an ordeal; she was desperately eager to see her leave.

"I am lousy in the part. You can tell me the truth," Sheila said dejectedly.

"It's just not right for you. I've had more experience working with the deaf."

"I'll never take another part where there's no speaking.

The first thing I'm going to do in New York is find a new agent. Manny doesn't take my career seriously."

"Are you ready to leave?"

"I suppose so. I won't have time to visit Springfield now. I'll have to get right back to New York and look for work."

Darcy shook her head sadly. "At least give Mom and Dad a call when you get there." She suddenly felt much older than her sister.

The rear exit of the theater was open, and the two attractive young women didn't leave the grounds unobserved.

CHAPTER NINE

Persuading Sheila to leave was the easy part. She still had to face Nick and the other cast members, all of whom had to be disappointed in her sister's poor performance. After transferring Sheila's luggage to the rented car, Darcy watched her drive away, then waited for half an hour before returning to the playhouse. Anyone who noticed the switch would assume she'd gone to get her own car from the garage where it had been serviced.

Sheila didn't hold grudges; she left willingly enough, telling Darcy that she'd been dreading an emergency rehearsal scheduled at two o'clock. Nick was going to try to doctor a sick play, and all his expertise would be focused on the character of Beth. Just the thought of being under that kind of pressure made Darcy breathlessly agitated, but she desperately wanted to give Nick a parting gift: a wonderful performance. It wouldn't atone for her terrible deceitfulness, but at least he might remember her with a granule of respect.

The time to tell him the truth was past; the only thing she could salvage from the whole bittersweet episode was the knowledge that she'd given everything she had to the role of the deaf woman.

After parking her car, she hurried to cabin six without being stopped, choosing to hide there until rehearsal time even though it meant skipping lunch. She was ravenously hungry again, but it was an emotional emptiness that craved a binge. Sucking on some peppermints she found at the bot-

160

tom of her purse, she reread the whole play, trying to psyche herself into the part. No one came to check on her reason for missing lunch, and she tried not to think about the tray Nick had carried through a rainstorm for her.

She'd forgotten to ask Sheila whether the rehearsal was in the lodge or the playhouse. Waiting until a minute before the hour, she stepped outside still wearing her new skirt and flowery blouse and waited to see if any cast members were visible. Raleigh and Sue ran toward the theater at the last minute, and she hurried after them.

Whatever she'd expected, it wasn't the awkward silence that fell over the other cast members when she walked down the ramp to the stage. Cole broke the stillness with a comment about a play he'd done on Broadway years ago, reasserting his need to be the center of attention, but not before Darcy received the message: everyone present was disappointed in her. Opening night had been a success, which only made the two performances following it all the more baffling.

Constance was glancing through a newspaper, not looking in Darcy's direction, and Raleigh began teasing Sue, talking a little too loudly to make up for the moment of strained silence. It hurt to feel the other players' rejection, but her worst fear was yet to be realized. Nick was nowhere in sight, and the additional waiting time was making her ill with anxiety. Whatever criticism he heaped on her, she deserved it as much as Sheila for getting involved where she didn't belong.

No one missed his entrance. He walked rapidly down the ramp, holding himself like a soldier on parade. In crisply pressed tan slacks and a white dress shirt, sleeves rolled and collar open, he looked all business, nothing like his usual casual self.

Darcy looked up at the ceiling fans, steadily moving warm air so the playhouse didn't become stifling, and down at her feet, unpolished toes showing between the straps of her sandals. She didn't know whether to be relieved or hurt when

Nick started organizing the rehearsal as though she didn't exist.

Leaning forward in a theater seat, she covered her face with her hands, doubled over in concentration, and tried to forget the other players and Nick. Her situation was almost unbearable, but she could handle it if she could channel all her insecurity into the part.

When she walked onto the stage for her first scene, she was Beth. At first Nick made a couple of suggestions, reminding her not to repeat things Sheila had done wrong during the performances, but he soon fell silent, becoming a spectator to the best run-through of the play she'd done.

Constance broke the ice at the end of Act II. "You must be feeling a lot better, Sheila."

"Yes, thank you."

"About Sunday," Constance said guardedly, "I never intended to give you advice you didn't want. Directing's not my job on this show."

Darcy could imagine her sister's reaction if Constance had offered counsel after the last disastrous performance. Impulsively she took Constance's hand. "I can't tell you how much your help has meant. Talking over the part with you was the best thing that happened in this play."

"Why, thank you." Even her acting experience couldn't mask Constance's confusion on hearing this sudden turnaround. She left the playhouse with a puzzled frown creasing her brow.

Darcy didn't want to be alone with Nick, but she wasn't quick enough to get away without his notice.

"Sheila, can I see you in my office, please?"

It was the last thing she wanted. Face to face with Nick, her courage might crumble. As angry as he was, he'd probably give her part to the first apprentice he saw if he learned about the deception.

"I'm—I'm not feeling well, I need to go to my cabin," she blurted out nervously.

"Then I'll walk you there." He caught up and walked beside her, keeping two feet of space between them.

"About your costume in—" he began.

"The red skirt is all wrong. I'll wear the same outfit I wore opening night."

"Why are you suddenly so cooperative?" he asked suspiciously.

"I just realize that Beth wouldn't wear such a foxy skirt." She could never act in a speaking part, she thought—there was a tremor in her voice that was beyond her control.

"No, she wouldn't. What I really want to know is what are you pulling?"

She was too wise to play dumb; Nick wasn't easily fooled. "I know I was terrible Saturday night and Sunday, but I feel better now. You won't have any complaints the rest of the week."

"I won't if you do as well as you did this afternoon. But your strategy won't work, Sheila. There's no part for you in my new play. Even if there was, I wouldn't cast you."

"I understand that. When this play closes, you'll never see me again." This was the saddest thing she'd ever said.

"It's a small world. Our paths may cross." He shrugged his shoulders and stepped aside so she could open the cabin door. "I see you've found your key. I'll take the spare back to the lodge."

"No! I mean, now I'm not sure where the spare is. I found one and lost the other."

Retrieving it from the bottom of Sheila's purse wasn't going to be easy; it was too much to hope that her sister had left it behind somewhere in the room.

"Something's wrong with you," he probed with narrowed eyes.

"No, I'm fine—now."

The perspiration on her forehead was cold. She couldn't look at Nick without yearning to be in his arms, but the gulf between them was impassable.

His eyes were observing her keenly, not missing a single detail from the black waves of hair fanning her cheeks to the small, neat ankles below her taut calves.

"You'd better stay fine!" he said grimly. "I can't understand. . . ." His voice trailed off with a perplexed frown. "Another performance like Saturday's or Sunday's . . ."

She knew exactly what he was trying to say. He thought Sheila's poor performances were deliberate acts of sabotage, done because he'd discouraged her interest in his new play.

"I have no reason not to do my best," she assured him.

"That's what I thought, but now . . . I'm just not sure how devious you are."

Blood rushed to her face as his remark hit home.

He turned away abruptly, walking rapidly back toward the theater but meeting Constance halfway there. The two huddled for several minutes as Darcy watched from her doorway, closing it when they separated.

Dinner loomed ahead like a trial by ordeal, and she thought of going somewhere alone in her car instead of braving the curiosity of the players at mealtime. Sheer stubbornness made her decide to eat at the lodge. She hadn't felt so persecuted since a gang of boys throwing snowballs had chased her home from school. Her friends had sneaked away on a safer but longer route when they spotted the boys, but Darcy stubbornly walked the way she always did, refusing to detour because of bullies. She arrived home battered and furious, her face cherry red from the snow they'd tossed at her. Sheila thought she was crazy; Darcy denied it, insisting on her right to walk home the way she always did. Surprisingly, the boys never tormented her again, although she walked through their territory alone or with friends for the rest of her years in elementary school.

She was walking the gauntlet again, entering the busy dining hall and picking up a tray to serve herself at the cafeteria-style counter beside the long window-opening between the kitchen and eating area. The table where Constance was sitting was full; Darcy found a seat at the far end of a table for six with only the lovebirds, Raleigh and Sue, at the other end.

Flaky whitefish served with Mrs. Corning's special wine sauce turned to sawdust in her mouth when she looked up to see Nick unloading his tray in the place opposite her.

"Do you mind?" he asked, seeing the panicky look on her face.

"No, of course not."

Sue stopped giggling and watched Nick spread out his knife, fork, and napkin, then arrange his dinner plate, salad bowl, and water glass with precise attention to their position.

"The fish is very good," Darcy said to break the heavy silence that had fallen on the diners at their table.

"Mrs. Corning is quite a cook. Do you do much cooking, Sheila?"

"Enough to survive." Another lie! Would they never end! Sheila was a lousy cook, but Darcy loved to experiment with new recipes, especially Chinese dishes loaded with crisp, delicately seasoned vegetables.

"Remember when you made that macaroni and cheese for me?" Nick asked.

"Yes, I guess so."

Darcy never fixed a casserole containing only starch and cheese. When she made a combination dish, it was loaded with lightly browned mushrooms, crispy onions, green peppers, tomatoes, and just a handful of pasta or rice.

"With Swiss cheese," he added. "Not many people make it that way."

The thought of a pale pan of pastelike pasta prepared by her sister zapped the last of her appetite.

"Of course, we really had fun when I grilled lamb chops," he said. "You pretended to love them, even though they had a quarter inch of charcoal on the outsides."

It was unlike Sheila to eat something just to be polite. Darcy frowned at him, not sure what to say.

"I talked to your agent," he said.

He did have her attention now. "When?"

"After rehearsal. He hasn't heard from you in quite a while."

"Does he have something for me?" Sheila would be sure to ask that question.

"I don't know. We talked about something else."

"Oh." Why mention it then? she wondered.

"The peace cobbler is good. Aren't you going to eat yours?"

"No, I guess not."

"Watching your weight?"

"Something like that."

"I thought you looked a little hippy in that red skirt."

"That's a good reason for not wearing it again."

"Yes, I suppose it is," he agreed. "If you don't want your cobbler . . ."

"No, take it, please."

"You know how hard I exercise every morning to wear off desserts. My favorite part of the meal."

"Have you been swimming every morning?" she asked.

"Yes, do you want to join me tomorrow?"

"No, I don't think so."

"So you haven't reformed; you don't like getting up early."

"If you'll excuse me . . ." What had made her think she was hungry enough to brave the dining hall?

"Wait. Keep me company while I finish. I like the way you did the park bench scene today. You won't make the same mistake you did Saturday, will you?"

"No, I won't react until David touches me." At least she knew what he was talking about in her sister's Saturday performance.

"I have to drive into Traverse City after dinner. The Cherry County Playhouse is going to rent us a few props we need for *Carousel*. Come with me."

"No, I'd rather not."

"An old friend of yours is there this week, Norm Hillard. I saw him last week, and he mentioned doing *Wings* with you in Connecticut. He was surprised you'd agreed to do it here. He didn't think it was your kind of play."

"I can't do *The Seven Year Itch* every summer."

The last thing she wanted was to meet someone else who knew her sister.

"I'd like to have Norm see you play Beth the way you did last Friday and this afternoon," Nick said thoughtfully. "Too bad his play opens this week."

The lush resort area was popular enough with summer people to support two theaters in a fifty-mile radius, but the Cherry County Playhouse featured bigger names.

"Too bad," Darcy said, hating herself for sounding so hypocritical.

"If you're sure you won't go with me . . ."

"No, I really would like to go to bed early."

"Then I'll send someone else, and we can swim later."

"Nick, I don't—"

"That's an order," he said curtly.

A moonlit swim with Nick was the last thing she needed. Waiting in her cabin, she didn't know how much more she could stand. He sent word with an apprentice at nine o'clock that he was still tied up, and it was after ten before he appeared at the cabin door wearing an unbuttoned shirt and his swimsuit. She'd been waiting restlessly in her suit for over an hour, hoping he'd change his mind but lacking the spirit to refuse him.

They weren't the only ones drawn to the lake on the balmy summer evening. Raleigh's and Sue's boisterous bantering could be heard before they reached the beach, and nearly the whole cast of *Carousel* was romping on the dock or in the shallows. Someone had launched the aging rowboat that belonged to the Duckeye, and it was manned now by amateurs noisily slapping the water with the oars but not getting anywhere.

"I've been wanting to swim straight across," Nick said.

Darcy saw the lights of summer cottages beckoning from the far side; the distance wasn't great, but she hadn't been swimming enough lately to have confidence in her endurance.

"It's a little too far for me, I think."

"That's okay. I don't want you in over your head."

Why did everything he say seem to have a double meaning? Feeling so tense that her muscles were rigid, Darcy flinched when he put his arm around her.

"I'm really not in the mood for much of a swim," she said when he pulled the towel from her shoulders.

"We could sit on the dock and talk," he suggested. "I think the party will break up soon. They have an early call in the morning."

"No, we're here, so we might as well swim," she said quickly.

Reluctantly letting her hand stay in his firm grip, she walked to the water's edge and stepped down from the sandy beach, submerging her legs to mid-calf in the chilly water. This time they waded slowly into deeper water, letting the swells lap their knees, thighs, and the edges of their suits. As the cold water crept up to her crotch and over her navel, she freed her hand and folded both arms over her chest, lagging behind when he plunged forward.

"Dive under. Get it over with," he urged.

Another step put the water level above her waist, and a gentle wave dampened the suit over her breasts.

"You're making it hard on yourself," he called with only his head visible above the dark sheen of the lake. "Trust me."

Again she read a second meaning into his words; if she didn't stop imagining things, she'd never survive the run of the play. With a quick kick she went under, putting distance between them as she veered off to the left.

She'd discounted his speed; surfacing, she found his face only a few feet from hers.

"The cottage near the boathouse is dark," he said. "It looks as if they haven't opened it for the summer yet. Let's swim there."

She didn't want to be alone with Nick on a deserted beach.

"Why would anyone with a cottage waste this lovely June weather? Maybe they've just gone to bed early."

"Come on. I'm not giving you a head start this time."

He paced her like a sheepdog herding its charge, never more than a few feet from her shoulder. She swam slowly, delaying the time when they'd swing their wet bodies onto the dry boards of the dock.

"You're holding back," he accused her, stopping ahead of her to tread water in her path.

"It's too cold to race."

"The air is warm." He let her pass and followed her the rest of the way to the tip of the duck's bill, putting his hands on her hips to help boost her to the dock.

"I wanted to be alone with you," he said, dripping beside her on the boards.

"Why?"

"Just to talk."

"Talk about what?" she asked suspiciously.

"Any subject you like."

Standing restlessly, she stepped from board to board, wary of splinters but liking the dry warmth of the wood underfoot.

"There's no boat in the water. That's a sure sign the cottage hasn't been opened yet," he said, following her toward shore.

"It seems a waste, not to use it in this perfect weather," she said.

"I imagine the owners are slaving away in some big, hot city so they can afford the place."

"You sound so cynical." The dock ended by a grassy bank, the growth underfoot high and prickly on her ankles.

"I'd hate to waste my life in a glass tower, glued to a chair all day," he said.

"I suppose some people prefer to work that way." She was wringing water from the ends of her hair, feeling the rivulets race down her back.

"What do you really want from life, Sheila?" His voice was too serious to give him a flip answer.

"I want to make other people happy, to help them." She knew Sheila would never give this answer, but she didn't care.

"By entertaining them?" He was standing dangerously close, carrying with him the clean scent of the northern lake.

"That's one way. I think we should go back. It's getting late."

"I like you this way," he said. "Away from the theater, talking quietly."

Did he have any idea what his closeness did to her? She stepped back onto the dock, but he was too fast, cutting off her retreat to the water by taking her in his arms and holding her there.

His lips were cold on her shoulder, sliding over her wet skin with more promise than passion, but when he found her mouth, they warmed. She didn't want his kiss to be so wonderful; she was afraid of the hot pulsations in her groin and the little convulsive shiver traveling down her spine.

Sliding her straps downward, he trailed his lips over the hard ridge of her collarbone and the smooth skin of her shoulder, not stopping until he peeled her suit to her waist and held the weight of both breasts in his cool palms. Tenderly, almost reverently, he ran the tip of his tongue over her hardened nipples, locking his hands on her hips.

"I hope your breasts never lose their rosy blush," he murmured, running his hands over her back.

Sheila must have lied! She couldn't believe the ardent man holding her had been indifferent to her sister all weekend.

"Stop, Nick!" Her voice came out as a hoarse whisper, and she lied to herself, pretending she didn't want him. "I'm going back."

"Let me hold you a minute. It was a long, empty weekend." He drew her closer, crushing her breasts against his smooth, hard chest.

"This isn't a good idea." Weak with relief, she still wasn't up to making love again under false pretenses.

"Isn't it?" He kissed her slowly. "A part in my new play isn't worth a few kisses?"

"No!"

She broke away, tortured by the real-life role she'd taken on herself. The truth was screaming for release, but she wouldn't give Nick a reason to order her away, not until the play was finished. Swimming with him was a terrible mistake. This was the last time she'd be a stand-in for Sheila in Nick's arms.

Running to the end of the dock, she dove into the water, pausing only long enough to return the straps to her shoulders. Swimming as though her life depended on it, she sliced through the black water, trying to pretend that Nick wasn't close beside her.

The other swimmers were gone. Nick reached the beach ahead of her, finding her towel and handing it to her. She didn't stop to dry off, not even feeling the gritty sand underfoot or the grass prickling her toes on her retreat to her refuge.

"Sheila?" His voice behind her held a question, but he didn't follow, watching instead from a distance until the cabin door closed behind her.

"Oh, Nick," she said aloud in her cabin, "why can't you see who I am?"

171

What did she expect him to see? she asked herself. Her face was her sister's, her voice, her hair, her build. The things that were uniquely Darcy's were buried in her heart. She was hoping for a miracle, a solution to an unsolvable dilemma. There was no way she could break free of the maze of lies and deceit she'd constructed. In the desolate wilderness of her soul, she only wanted to start over again with Nick, to have a chance at his love for herself.

It was hopeless. He looked at her and remembered all her sister had done to hurt him. Even his kisses were a form of revenge; he didn't want to be in love with Sheila. Darcy was sure he'd hate both of them when she told him the truth, after the play closed.

CHAPTER TEN

Darcy was losing weight, and the dark purple shadows under her eyes owed nothing to makeup. Staying in bed instead of going to breakfast, she hoped to snatch a little more sleep after a restless night of disturbing dreams. Blaming the lumpy mattress and the bright sun streaming through one window, she finally gave up. Somehow she had to get through a long day with nothing much to do until curtain time.

With time hanging heavily on her hands, she went to the playhouse to see if she could be useful in some way. Producing a musical in-the-round required special creativity, and the set designer was the hero of the production. There was nothing she could do to help finish the multilevel set, but she did volunteer to hem some costumes that were being adjusted to fit cast members.

Pricking her finger for the third time as she absentmindedly manipulated a needle, she couldn't keep her attention from wandering to the main backstage working area, visible through the open entrance of the wardrobe. Nick was nowhere in sight.

Important as the play was to Darcy, she finally admitted the truth: returning had everything to do with Nick. For his sake, she didn't want *Wings of Love* to be a flop. She loved him.

Carrying a bright yellow dress with her, she went into the theater where the set for the first and last scene of *Wings* was set up. It was the living room of Beth's home, a setting with heavy, masculine furniture that reflected the domination of her father: a massive caramel-colored leather couch, borrowed from a local business; a smoking stand, veneered on the outside and copper-lined inside; a giant ottoman; a tweed recliner; and a commercially-made brown braided rug. Darcy sat on the long couch, looking at the deserted stage and running the needle in and out of the pinned hem.

She knew what she had to do. With six more performances scheduled, the run of *Wings* was too long to keep her secret. Nick had to know the truth, even if he banned her from the play as a fraud. She wasn't an equity actor, and there was no valid excuse for her to be part of the cast. Losing the opportunity to finish the role of Beth would hurt terribly, but continuing the deception was impossible.

Tying off the thread at the end of the finished hem, she went to look for Nick, wanting to get through the ordeal of telling him as soon as possible.

"Ken, have you seen Nick?" she asked, cornering the stage manager as he talked to one of the technicians.

"Not since breakfast. He went into Traverse City."

"Will he be gone all day?"

"He shouldn't be."

He was. Napping on a towel beside the lake, she got up several times, checking to see if his car was back. Not until dinner did he return, and then Darcy found it impossible to speak to him alone. She hadn't noticed how popular he was with the cast and crew, many of whom seemed to hang on every word he said, especially the fledgling actors. Only Cole was indifferent to the director, but he showed his approval by occasionally talking man-to-man with Nick, as though he were Cole's only equal at the Duckeye.

Her mind went blank ten minutes before the opening curtain, but well-rehearsed responses saved the evening. She managed to make her entrance at the right time, and, once on stage, she slowly became Beth again, feeling her way into the emotions of the young deaf girl. The park bench scene left the audience entranced; their approval at the end of Act I was overwhelming.

There was no opportunity to talk to Nick between acts. She wasn't imagining things; he was avoiding her.

At the end of the play, the audience's applause was thunderous. She wished it meant more to her, but all she could think about was what she'd say when she was finally alone with Nick.

"Weeknight crowds are usually more reserved," Nick said, following her through the curtained exit. "Most of that was for you."

"Nick." Now that she had his attention, a crippling shyness made talking to him seem unbearable. "Can I see you?"

"I'm here." He spread his hands to emphasize the obvious.

"No, I mean alone."

"I have to go out front and say hello to some friends of my parents who're passing through on their vacation. They'll want to buy me a drink, so I may not be back until late."

"I'll wait."

"You look tired. Maybe you should get to bed early."

She shook her head, numb with misery. If she didn't say what had to be said, there wouldn't be any sleep for her that night.

"When I get back I have a few things to clear up in my office. If you're still awake, you can find me there."

Back at her cabin she took a long shower and dressed in a white wraparound skirt and a sleeveless gold top. Across the way the playhouse was deserted, with only a dim night-light showing in the work area.

Wandering to the beach, she found a few of the cast and crew in the water, refreshing themselves after another long day. With no inclination to join them, she walked along the water's edge, beyond the boundary of the playhouse property, slowly making her way past a wooded area and toward the shoreline that formed the bill of the imaginary duck. The distance by foot was longer than swimming to the cottage near the yellow boathouse, but walking made the wait to see Nick more tolerable.

The cottage was dark again, and she regretted the owner's wastefulness, letting lovely summer days slip by while the little retreat stayed vacant. The dock creaked under the soft slap of her sandals, and she looked down on the calm surface of the water, a shimmering mirror under the pale glow of a nearly full moon. Her life seemed much like the cottage—empty and wasted.

Returning more hurriedly, she found the beach deserted, but the rear interior of the theater was bright with light, signaling Nick's return with a warm yellow glow.

Entering the workroom, she pushed the heavy door—left open for her, she was sure—until the lock clicked into place. Trying not to think of *The Phantom of the Opera*, she slowly moved toward the office, coming face to face with a closed door. Her knock was so timid and tentative he might not have heard it. Instead of repeating her summons, she slowly edged the door open and stepped into the dark room, afraid that she'd misjudged the signal light from the entrance.

"You didn't go to bed." His voice was only a husky whisper that came from the darkness.

"No."

As her eyes adjusted to the dark, she saw him sitting beside the desk, the chair tipped back on two legs. Righting it with a loud clunk on the concrete, he reached toward his breast pocket, but there was nothing there. Did he still instinctively reach for the long-absent cigarettes because he, too, was uneasy? Darcy held her breath, not knowing how to begin.

"You were lovely tonight. In your part." His voice was a caress that made it even harder for her to speak.

"Thank you," she murmured.

"What I don't understand," he said rising to his feet, "is why you were so different Saturday and Sunday. Can you explain?"

"Yes." Her throat was like sandpaper. "Yes, I can now."

He moved closer, almost overwhelming her. "I'd really like to know," he said, touching her cheek with the back of one finger.

"Can I start at the beginning?"

"Whatever you like."

"My sister had a terrible problem. She thought her career would be ruined if she didn't fulfill a contract. She came to me for help. Maybe I should've refused, but I didn't."

"She couldn't handle her own obligations?"

"If she did, she might miss a wonderful opportunity, a turning point."

"In her career?"

"Yes, she needed my help desperately."

"You didn't want to do as she asked?"

"No." The lump in her throat made it difficult to speak. "But I wanted something from her."

"Something important to you?"

"I guess so. I wanted her to spend some time with our parents this summer. They really miss her."

"So, Sheila, you agreed to do a favor for your sister." He emphasized *Sheila*.

"Darcy."

"Darcy?"

"I'm Darcy. Sheila is my twin. I agreed to stand in for her so she could go to California. It was terribly important to her to follow up on a possible film role."

"Is acting your profession?" His voice was flat, telling her nothing.

"No, I'm a speech pathologist. I work in the Springfield schools. Sheila thought I could play the part of Beth because there wasn't any talking. I know sign language; I worked at a camp for deaf children for three summers."

"But Sheila never did?"

"No."

"And she thought all you'd have to do was stand around and look like her?" Anger was creeping into his voice now.

"That's what she said. It didn't work out to be quite so simple. She didn't know you'd be here."

"I'm sure she didn't," he said dryly. "Did Sheila get a part in a film?"

"No. She came here and switched places with me Saturday."

"Don't bother telling me why. I have a pretty good idea what Sheila wanted from me. What I don't understand is why you're here now instead of her."

"I made her leave."

"You made her?" Finally he sounded surprised. "Why?"

"I saw *Wings* Saturday night. She was ruining it!"

"And that bothered you?" He turned on a small desk lamp, studying her in the dim glow.

"Yes, terribly. The cast didn't deserve what she was doing to it. She just didn't care about the play. Sheila likes comedy, funny lines and—"

"Yes, I know what Sheila likes," he said with heavy irony. "You came back to save the play? Was that your only reason for returning, Darcy?"

Hearing him say her own name for the first time made her feel weepy, but she forced herself to be wholly truthful, regaining a little of her self-respect as the webs of deceit fell away.

"No, I wanted to see you again."

"Ah." He expelled breath and let a heavy silence grow between them.

"Now you know," she said miserably. "I'll leave in the morning."

"I'm only beginning to hear everything I want to know. What makes you think I'll let you leave?"

"Let me? I thought . . ."

178

"That I'd fire you if I knew the truth?"

She nodded unhappily.

"We still have a play to finish, a good play."

"I really want to finish it," she whispered.

"Let's go back to where you said you wanted to see me again." He slowly bent his head, finding her lips for a long, tender kiss. "About wanting to see me . . ."

His hands were heavy on her shoulders as he waited for something more from her.

"I did want to see you," she said softly, still wondering at his reaction. So far he didn't seem angry or terribly surprised.

"Oh?" He wasn't going to help her.

"I . . . I care about you."

"That's nice." His voice told her nothing, but he rewarded her with a lingering kiss, sweet and undemanding.

Tossing aside pride and common sense, she clung to him. The taste of his mouth was sweet torture to her senses. When he lifted his head and looked down on her, she felt diminished in his eyes. Was his kiss a parting act of charity? Still holding her close, he patted her head, a gesture that was neither comforting nor reassuring.

"I love you, Darcy," he said so softly she thought it was her feverish imagination conjuring up the words.

"You can't. You love Sheila."

"I could love Sheila," he said soberly, keeping her in the circle of his arms, "if she were giving and loving like her sister, if she didn't let her ambition possess her, if she didn't use people to get what she wants."

"She's not all bad!"

"No, she isn't. I thought I loved her once. I hated myself for being attracted to her again. Let me show you something."

He twisted the gooseneck on the desk lamp so it focused on his hands. Picking up a manila envelope, he opened it and took a slip of paper from a sheaf held by a rubber band.

"Read this," he said handing it to her.

"The part of Beth will be played by Darcy Simmons," she read in astonishment. "Nick, what is this?"

"An insert for the programs. I had them printed today."

"Then you knew! How long?" She stared at the paper, then searched his face.

"When did I suspect or when was I sure?"

"Either! Both!"

"I wondered at the change in Sheila from the beginning. At first I thought she was giving the performance of her life, trying to convince me to use her in the new play. But I didn't think she was talented enough to make me believe she cared about me. If she was, why were the first rehearsals so bad? Was she trying to convince me she could improve in any part if she tried?"

"Then you knew all along I wasn't Sheila?"

"No." He shook his head gravely. "I wanted to believe Sheila could change, that she could be everything I wanted her to be. You see, I was falling in love, and this time it was different from anything I'd ever experienced."

"I feel so terrible. I hated pretending to be Sheila!"

He took the slip of paper from her hand, dropping it on the desk with the envelope, then reached out to stroke her cheek with the backs of his fingers. His tenderness made her eyes tear, and when he kissed her, she parted her lips in welcome, still afraid to believe that he loved her, not Sheila. His kiss was unlike any other, sweet almost beyond endurance because it was meant for her. He knew who she was and he loved her.

With one hand she gripped the edge of the desk, needing to touch something solid as proof that it was really happening, that she was in Nick's arms and he cared for her. A small calendar, twelve tiny months set in a cardboard frame, bent under her grasp and fell to the floor when the need to touch him overruled everything else.

"Darcy, darling Darcy." He held her closer, doing wonderful things to her ear.

"How did you know my name?" She stepped back, searching his face but unable to see his expression in the shadowy light.

"I didn't. Sheila never talked about her family. I didn't even know she had a twin."

"But . . ."

He kissed her then perched on the edge of the desk, holding her shoulders to keep her close. "Let me finish. When Sheila took your place, she was indifferent to the rest of the cast. She didn't even seem to know Constance, and I knew the two of you had become friends."

"And she wanted to change Beth's costumes."

"She did change them without asking anyone, sending Fran into a tizzy."

"You let her!"

"I wanted to find out what was happening. Suddenly you, or rather she, was acting like the Sheila I'd known before. Nothing seemed right. What she did to the play was unbelievable!"

"It isn't her kind of play," Darcy defended her twin weakly.

"She doesn't have the slightest empathy for a character like Beth. When you stepped into the part at rehearsal yesterday, I remembered seeing someone with her, a woman about the same age and build in a phony-looking blond wig."

"You weren't close enough to recognize a wig!"

"Hindsight, darling." He squeezed both of her hands, keeping them in his. "Then I only knew something was wrong. I knew a person couldn't be so completely different from one day to the next. Either you were a multiple personality or a twin. Thank heavens, you're a twin."

"How did you find out for sure?"

"A little telephone detective work. I called Manny

Zwarles, who's a friend of mine besides being Sheila's agent. He gave me your parents' address. Your mother was very helpful after she was convinced I was a friend of Sheila's. She volunteered more than I needed to know."

"She would." Darcy smiled. It was just beginning to sink in that there was forgiveness and, more important, love in his expressive eyes.

"She would enjoy a visit from your sister." He brought her hand to his lips and kissed each knuckle in turn.

"You're not angry?" Her knees were shaking, and she still couldn't believe his reaction.

"I'm furious." He kissed her chin and the tip of her nose, trapping her between his legs.

"You'll never trust me." She had to give voice to the worst of her fears. "You can't be sure I'm not like my sister."

"You're wrong. I know how persuasive Sheila can be when she wants something. My worst worry has been that you wouldn't admit the truth. That you'd leave without saying anything."

"I couldn't." She reached up to touch the soft waves of hair on the sides of his head, cupping his ears and rubbing the lobes with her thumbs, letting the joy of the last few minutes sink in.

"You love me for myself," she whispered in awe.

He heard the wonderment in her voice and slid off the desk, pulling her closer. "Believe me, I do."

In the history of kisses, there wasn't a sweeter one. Her lips tingled as warm waves of desire rose up within her, at last letting her relax in his arms. For long, delicious moments nothing existed but his mouth on hers. Whispering her name over and over again, testing the rhythm and rightness of it, he slid his hands slowly down her back, coming to rest on the firm, sleek roundness of her bottom.

Swept into his arms, she clung to his neck, nuzzling his throat and moaning soft endearments, stunned by a joy she'd never expected.

"We've wasted too much time," he said, taking her hand and stepping into the darkened theater.

There was just enough light seeping in from the work-room to guide them to the stage, where he took her in his arms again.

"It's too late for rehearsing," she said breathlessly.

"We don't need it. This is opening night for us, darling."

He found the tie that held her wraparound skirt, letting it fall to the canvas floor, sliding his hands under her panties to seductively knead the soft flesh.

"If I needed proof," he said with a husky sigh, "it's here. Your sister is getting a big rear."

"You didn't—"

"No." He laughed wickedly. "All I did was observe."

Her panties fell to her ankles, and she kicked them aside, quivering when he peeled off her top and fondled her breasts with the sensitive pads of his fingers. As his tender, questing hands explored more and more of her, she didn't know how she could contain her love without bursting. Slowly she un-buttoned his shirt, stripping it away from his warm, firm shoulders and dropping it to the floor. Wiggling her toes out of her sandals, she bent to untie his shoes, glad when he became impatient and shed the rest of his clothing himself.

The light filtering in through the curtain over the back-stage entryway created shadowy images, spooky when Nick suddenly left her.

"Don't move," he ordered.

She watched until his naked form was lost in the dusky interior of the theater, gasping when a sudden beam of light, a single spot, softly illuminated the massive caramel couch. High above on the catwalk that frightened her, Nick waved to her, moving pantherlike in his nakedness. Her heart was in her throat until he was in her arms again, holding her so tight that the furious beating of her heart seemed to rock them both.

"You frighten me when you go up there."

"I want to see the woman I love."

He led her to the couch, pulling her onto his lap as dust motes danced in the misty atmosphere high above them. In the soft golden light that hit them, his face was softer, his long lashes a feathery fringe that tickled her eyelids. Sliding to her back, she drew him into her arms, willing away all thoughts of her sister, parting her lips, welcoming him with her whole heart. He hovered over her, blanketing her skin with hungry kisses, memorizing every curve and swell of her body until their mutual longing rose to a boiling point.

"Darcy." He said her name again and again, reminding her that his love was all hers, just as she was his.

"The light," she said, looking upward and covering her eyes, drawing him nearer to be her shield.

"I love you, Darcy."

"I love you." Her voice was hoarse with longing. "I love you, Nick."

Closing her eyes in total abandonment, she received him with a wild cry of joy, digging her fingers into his back, his straining shoulders, his hot, slippery buttocks. Around them the ghosts of past audiences applauded their perfect consummation, but Darcy could only hear the roaring of her own secret sea and the words of love that truly belonged to her now. She was soaring, clasping him against her trembling thighs, riding the warm, rushing tide that wiped out the last of her doubts. Locking her legs and arms around him, she delighted in the crush of his body, his weight not a burden but tangible proof of her incredible good fortune. He loved her; he loved her!

"I never knew spotlights could be so hot," he murmured, leaning on his elbows and looking at her with love written on every line of his face.

"I don't want you to go up there again." She eyed the high bridge with apprehension.

"It's my second home," he assured her. "I had to have light to see you."

184

Watching him dress and climb another time to the high perch, she waited and tried to believe they could never be separated by time, space, or the death of their love, but what would happen when the play ended, as all plays did? Her life was in Springfield; he belonged to a glamorous, exciting world she'd only glimpsed from the sidelines. Her dreamlike euphoria faded as she dressed in the darkness, waiting for her surefooted lover.

"Let's go back to my cabin," he said, rejoining her, holding her, not for a moment willing to deprive himself of the softness of her body or the sweet scent of her hair in his nostrils.

"I can't believe we did this," she said self-consciously. "What if someone had come?"

"I'd say we were rehearsing a new play," he teased, "but I know the door locked when you shut it."

"No one would believe we were rehearsing!" She playfully pushed him away.

"I was. I was rehearsing for a new life."

She held her breath, not daring to believe his implication.

"I asked you once to stay the rest of the summer," he said gravely, pulling her to the couch in the near dark, sitting beside her and taking both of her hands in his.

"I wanted so badly to say yes!"

"Say it now then."

She hesitated, knowing that she never wanted to leave him, but understanding herself too well to give the answer he wanted. A summer romance would never be enough for her, not when she loved Nick the way she did.

"I don't know if I can."

"I'm not going to give you a choice."

"Oh?" She pulled her hands away.

"I don't want one of those marriages where the husband lives on the East Coast and the wife in the midwest."

On the darkened stage the couch creaked under her but nothing seemed real. She didn't know what to say.

"Before you say yes," he said, leaning over to brush a kiss on her cheek, "I have to tell you the truth."

"What?" She imagined the worst: a wife still in his life.

"Sheila never cooked anything for me, certainly not macaroni and cheese. I don't like lamb chops, grilled or any other way, and I only eat desserts so Mrs. Corning's feelings won't be hurt. For some reason she thinks I'm addicted to cherry crunch."

"You were testing me to see if I'd confess?"

"A little more detective work. Will you forgive me and marry me?"

"I want to."

"But?"

"I don't want to give up my work."

"Darling, people have speech problems in New York. I've even been accused of having a slight nasal twang! If that's the only thing . . ."

"No. We haven't known each other very long. You don't know my parents. . . ."

"I'll love them like my own."

"And Sheila will be your sister-in-law."

He took a deep breath. "I can't hate anyone who brought us together. She'll never be in a play of mine, but maybe I can find something for her with a friend of mine who's doing a made-for-TV movie in California. I like the idea of keeping my sister-in-law on the other side of the country."

"I'm glad you don't hate her. I can't turn off my love for her, even though she does things I don't like."

"Just so long as you never turn off your love for me." He stood and offered her his hand.

"I won't," she vowed quietly.

She stood on tiptoes, holding his face between her hands, and sealed her promise with a long, deep kiss.

"If you ever want a new profession," he said, wrapping his arms around her, "you can be an understudy for any play I direct."

"No, I never want to be a stand-in again. After *Wings of Love* you'll have to be content with a backstage wife."

"I will be," he promised, hugging her to his side as they walked down the exit ramp.

LAURA LONDON

Let her magical romances enchant you with their tenderness.

For glorious, romantic storytelling at its very best, get lost in these novels of 19th century London.

____ A HEART TOO PROUD... 13498-6 $2.95

____ THE BAD BARON'S
DAUGHTER 10735-0   2.95

____ THE GYPSY HEIRESS......... 12960-5   2.95

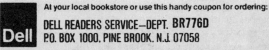